Good Girl

A STONEBRIDGE DADDIES COLLECTION

NATALIE KNIGHT

Copyright © 2022 by Natalie Knight

All rights reserved.

No part of this book may be reproduced in any form or by any electronic or mechanical means, including information storage and retrieval systems, without written permission from the author, except for the use of brief quotations in a book review.

Cover Designed by Cormar Covers

*To all the women who love a little positive reinforcement
*wink wink**

Daddy's Good Girl

CHAPTER 1
Past Wounds ~ Olivia

"OPEN THE FUCKING DOOR, OLIVIA," Damien spat.

I sliced my gaze to the shaking coffee table perched up against the front door as I packed my duffel bag. I didn't care about the furniture or the photos. I only cared about getting the last of my things out to my car and getting the hell out of there in one piece. The banging subsided, and I stilled my movements, placing one foot in front of the other at a sloth-like pace as I made my way from the bedroom to the living room. The strap to my duffle dug into the flesh of my shoulder, and although the sensation of a heavy bag was always annoying, it stung worse this time.

"Fuck, Olivia!" he yelled once more.

The round vase on the coffee table toppled off the edge and rolled to the center of the room. Oreo circled it and placed her tiny paw on top of the colorful vase. I thought Damien was going to knock the door down. I was sure of it. He had no issues applying force to things. He made sure I knew that.

"C'mon, baby. I promise I'll never do anything to hurt you again. You're overreacting. Let's just talk."

Lies. Our entire relationship was soaked in paint and dried in a coat of hurtfulness. I was tired of the pain, the physical and the emotional. The cracks in my heart and the splinter in my soul weighed me down, and although when I looked into Damien's eyes, a flicker of hope teased me, I knew that light would die out, that it wouldn't last. Because it never did. Oreo circled my ankles, and I picked her up and set her on the couch. The banging stopped, and Damien powered down the stairs and out of the front door of the building. A sigh of relief washed over me when the engine of his truck started up, and I peeked out of the window.

I'm officially single and staying off the market for the rest of my life. Oreo purred before jumping into my arms. I set her down on the coffee table and geared up my strength before pushing it away from the door. Just like the queen she was, Oreo sat and watched as a row of sweat broke across my forehead. I let my arms drop heavily to my side. I picked up the duffle and scooped Oreo into my arms. Taking one last glance at the place I had called home for the previous two years,

I placed the key on the kitchen counter and opened the front door.

"OUT OF ALL THE places we could have gotten lunch, you choose the coffeehouse you work at?" Mia plopped down into the chair and reached for her favorite drink.

"I know, but they have the best gingersnap cookies, and I get a discount because I work here."

She sipped her coffee with squinted eyes as she peered in my direction. Mia begged to have lunch with me today. All I wanted to do was crawl into bed and turn on *The Witcher* as I stuffed cheese cream bagel bites between my lips. Guilty pleasure.

"How did it go? I'm so sorry I couldn't be there with you. Fucking traffic." She grabbed my hand and relayed a soft smile.

Mia's been my best friend since high school. Our acquaintance was like fate. I had cookies, and she had Nutella. It was a friendship match made in heaven.

I took a sip of my matcha green tea and breathed. "It was okay. I thought he would knock down the door, but the coffee table came in handy."

"Ugh. I hope he gets hit by a bus or drowns, or for fuck sake, maybe a pack of hyenas will find him."

"I don't think there are any hyenas in Stonebridge." I snorted.

"Dream big girlie, anything is possible. Anywho, onward and upward." She raised her coffee cup and clanked it against mine.

Even in the worse of situations, she knew exactly how to make me feel better. That was her gift. She was the light that I needed when dreariness surrounded me.

"So, how's the apartment decorating coming along? Did you—"

"Umm, hey. " A voice interrupted Mia mid-sentence. We both turned to find a tall slim guy around our age standing at the side of our table.

"Yeah?" Mia asked as she tapped her nails on the table.

"What's up? I was checking you out, and you're cute. I'm throwing a party tonight. I can text you details if you're free."

Being the positively optimistic mermaid Mia was, she perked up like a fresh pot of coffee.

"We'll love too—"

"Oh, just you. No offense. You're not the type my friends go after," he said as he locked his gaze on my plus size curves.

Ouch. I rolled my eyes and pulled my phone out of

my purse. The entire coffeehouse went silent once Mia told him off at the top of her lungs. I didn't know if I wanted to chime in, clap, or run and hide.

"That wasn't necessary," I whispered.

She folded her arms across her chest and tilted her head. "It was. He's just another douche bag with a cock between his legs and air in his brain."

I shoved a bit of gingersnap past my lips and chewed slowly and continued on answering her previous question. "Well, it's shitty, has old paint, the floor creaks when I walk on it, and I'm positive my neighbor is a vampire due to all the garlic she uses, but it's mine. All mine."

"It will take some time to adjust to being on your own, but this is good for you. You don't deserve to be with such a sleazeball." She finished the rest of her coffee.

I placed my elbows on the table and pressed my palms into my cheeks. "Now, if only I could find a better paying job."

The whites of Mia's eyes widened with excitement. "I totally brain farted. I saw this post when I was combing through the incoming job posts. I'll text you the link."

My phone chimed, and I pulled it out of my purse. Trying to curb my enthusiasm, I opened the link and read the post. "An executive assistant? I can't even keep my life organized, let alone someone else's."

"Faith, my child. Also, you'll be getting a package tonight. A special home warming gift from yours truly." She jogged her eyebrows up her forehead with a goofy look on her face.

"Oreo has too many toys as it is. I'm running out of room." I let my words trail off and finished the last of my coffee.

"Call me later." She stood and slid her arms through her thin jacket.

I waved bye and leaned back in the chair, taking in the comforting sound of chatter and the grinding of the coffee machine. I really did like working at the coffeehouse, but it didn't pay enough, and now that I was on my own with literally zero savings, I needed a job that would help me get back on my feet.

"Hey, Olivia," my manager called.

I raised a brow at her request, and my shoulder slumped. I had a feeling she was going to ask me if I could work for a few hours. Although it wasn't super crowded, it was a lot for one barista and a manager who didn't know how to work the new espresso machine. She reeled me in with a promise that she'd pay me overtime for my four hours, and in a blink of an eye, I was putting on my apron and tying my hair into a bun—the broke life of Olivia Mason.

With my back to the counter, I casually told the customer demanding my attention that I would be with them in a second. Then my stomach released a swarm of butterflies, and my words turned to mush. He repeated his coffee order once more and pulled a $50 bill from his wallet. I stood there like a deer in headlights, my movements slowing to a crawl. I didn't know what was happening to me and why I couldn't pry my eyes away from the hazel ones in front of me.

"Are you going to make my coffee, or do I have to go behind the counter and make it myself?"

I swallowed and grabbed a large cup from the tower next to me. Counting down the seconds until the machine stopped, I took another glance in his direction and regretted it almost instantly. His glare was so strong I was certain he knew every thought running through my brain. I plopped the top on his cup and slid over to him.

"Keep the change." Refusing to break our gaze, he snatched the coffee and turned toward the door.

CHAPTER 2
Office Grump ~ Aiden

THE NEXT DAY

FUCK, who the hell parked near my spot? Didn't they know not to park their shit car next to the spot clearly marked CEO? I killed the engine and opened the door. Sliding my badge across the keypad, my private elevator chimed, and the doors slid back. All chatter seemed to cease when the heel of my leather loafers sounded off the marble flooring. I own a small private security firm with less than 50 employees. I didn't need a huge company with thousands of employees to stake my claim in Stonebridge. My work and that of my employees spoke for themselves. Even without an elaborate team, I had the liberty of providing security to some of Stonebridge's most elite.

Stopping me in my tracks, the head of HR rambled in my ears about the required paperwork for one of my workers. I winged a brow before snatching the file out of his hand. Whatever words were tethering off the edge of his lips, he swallowed them back down and turned on his heels. I wasn't one to care about what people thought of me, but the company's rumor mill didn't escape me. They coined me the grumpy CEO, and just thinking about it had my mouth morphing into a smile. It didn't hurt my feelings; it actually made me happy. People don't bore me with their mundane and useless stories about their weekends and shit holidays.

Silence greeted me as I pushed open the door to my office, and I blew out a breath. Then, jonesing for a nice tall cup of coffee, I rounded my desk and pressed the call button.

"Who are you calling? You have no assistant. Remember?" My brother swiveled around in the plush chair nestled in the corner overlooking the Stonebridge skyline.

I rolled my eyes and sank into my chair. He was right. I didn't have an assistant because I fired them all for getting my coffee order incorrect.

"Well, you know me. One strike, and you're out." I flipped open my laptop and pressed my finger onto the reader. Jasper took a big bite out of the apple he was tossing in the air and made sure to annoy me with his obnoxious chewing.

"Really? Just because they don't remember your exact coffee order?"

"What can I say? I like a closed mouth and open ears. Is that such a bad thing?"

He pinched the bridge of his nose and raised his chin to the ceiling, an audible sigh pushing past his lips. "You know why I'm here, right?"

"Yup, and nope." I deadpanned.

Jasper leaned in and placed his elbows on his thighs. I swiveled around to face him. Like clockwork, he was here to ask me if I wanted to go to the annual private security and technology convention. I always said no when he asked. Nothing irritated my soul more than a forced conversation with other security company CEOs who only wanted to know the names on your client list.

"I go every year. Alone. I'm running out of excuses to tell people when they ask why you aren't there."

I leaned back in my chair and raised an ankle to my leg. "Then don't lie. Tell them I'm working."

He stood and perched his ass on the corner of my desk. He always gives me a hard time, but his annoyance toward my solitude and isolation increased over the past few years. Ever since my divorce six years ago, he's been trying to push me back into my pre-marriage state. Except, spending all night out drinking in bars just to wake up groggy with a pounding headache the next day wasn't my idea of fun anymore. It was more like torture. I created a wall around my heart after my ex-wife broke it, and I had no intention of letting anyone in. Ever.

I'd put all of my frustrations into expanding my security business once the dust of my long and drawn-out divorce settled.

He raised his hands in the air and lowered his chin. "I get it. You're a hermit who doesn't like people, but you have to come to the convention this year."

"Why?" I folded my arms across my chest.

"Because the vendor for that new security technology will be there, and they're looking for beta testers, but you have to be there in person to sign up."

Shit. He had a point. I've been eyeing some new software, and from what I've heard, it's going to be hard to get my hands on it once it's released. Getting on the beta team would reserve my purchasing spot once it's on the market.

I teetered my head from side to side and let out a breath. "Fine, but you're going with me."

"Perfect." He clapped his hands together.

My phone beeped, and I answered. The front desk let me know my 10:30 a.m. interview was here. I stood and closed the top of my laptop.

Jasper walked over to the door and pulled it open. "Don't you use a temp agency to hire assistants?"

"I did. But I need someone who knows how to read a calendar. Apparently, the temp agency doesn't check for that little detail."

"Go easy on this one, eh?" he said before walking into the hallway.

I pulled my tablet from my drawer and opened up the email with all the interviewees information. *Olivia Mason.*

CHAPTER 3
Daddy Material~Olivia

ONCE I LEFT the coffeehouse yesterday I went straight home to fill out the application for the job Mia told me about. To my surprise someone from HR called me at 8 a.m. this morning. The woman on the other line of the phone said that the CEO was in desperate need of an assistant and asked if I would be willing to come in for an interview this morning. The phone screening was brief, and luckily, I was able to answer a few simple questions.

Oreo peered up at me as she circled my feet. I spent all morning rummaging through my clothing in search of something decent to wear. Moving into my new shitty apartment drained what little savings I had and swiping my credit card wasn't much of an option either since I'd maxed it out. Feeling like I struck gold when I spotted a black pencil skirt and a cream-colored blouse near the back of my closet, I snatched them off the hangers and tossed them on the bed.

"Well, what do you think?" I swirled on my heels toward Oreo, who was too busy licking her paws to be interrupted.

I smoothed out my skirt and prayed to the stocking goddess that the waistband wouldn't roll down. Gliding the brush through my tresses once more, I put a fresh coat of gloss on my lips and headed out the door.

The drive over was swift. Stonebridge didn't have hectic traffic like the big city that was located three hours away, and I was thankful. I parked in one of the visitor's spots in front of the building and swallowed my resolve as I headed toward the glass doors in the distance. My little car stood out like a neon peacock among the luxury vehicles. The bottom of my flats glided beneath the shiny tile, and I stopped in front of the information desk.

Fussing with my wallet, I shoved my driver's license back inside and followed the guard to the silver elevators. He swiped the key card and gave me a dismissive nod as the door shut. I closed my eyes and counted to ten as I tried to calm my nerves. *It's fine. You're going to do great, and if not, there's a broken espresso machine calling your name.*

"Getting off?" a man asked.

I nodded, not realizing the doors had opened, and hurried past him.

"Good luck," he said as he wiggled his brows.

The hallway was mostly quiet, with only a few conversations coming from open office doors. The man at the front desk told me that the interviewer was ready for me and to wait outside the door. Nearing the end of the hall, I stopped in front of a large, frosted glass door. Unsure if I should wait, I extended my arm to knock when the door swung open. The greeting that I practiced all morning dissolved on my tongue, leaving me with a pile of jumbled syllables.

A man with steel gray hair and penetrating hazel eyes stood before me. My spine melted at the sight of him, and my brain fogged. He quirked a brow and turned on his heels. With my movements frozen, I tracked his leopard-like grace across the room. I wondered if he remembered me from the coffee shop the other day. *Probably not.* The only people who remember me are bill collectors and my crazy ex.

"Are you going to come in, or do you want me to interview you from the hallway?" His voice's smooth yet deep baritone made my pulse jab in my neck.

I stepped from the hard tile onto the soft carpet and eyed the two large chairs sitting in front of his desk. His titan shoulders and barrel chest filled out the fabric of his shirt, which became tight around the biceps as he extended his arm, motioning me to take a seat.

"Resume?" he asked.

I slipped my fingers into my purse, retrieving a folded piece of paper, and slid it over as I avoided his gaze. Forgetting to remove my hand, the pads of his fingers brushed against mine, and I snapped my hand back when a surge of electricity surged between us. He leaned back in his chair, and I placed my hands in my lap. Lances of sunlight seeped in through the wide windows.

I waited draped in a veil of silence. The temptation to chew on the inside of my jaw possessed me, and I swallowed down the coppery taste of blood that trickled on my tongue. The top of my resume cut off just below his eyes, and I hated I didn't look away in time before our gaze locked once more.

Lifting a brow, he shifted and lowered my resume to the desk. "You have no experience, you're highly unqualified, and there's a stain on the corner of your resume."

He slid my resume back over, and I stuffed it back into my purse. Gearing up to thank him for his time, I stood, but the look on his face made me sit back down.

"Unfortunately, I'm desperate, and I don't have time to keep interviewing candidates. So, do you know how to read a calendar?"

I stilled my movements before nodding.

"Good. Do you have a good memory?"

I nodded again and slowly leaned back into the chair.

"Can you start now?"

"Um, well. I have a shift at the coffeehouse later today and—"

"A medium americano with an extra shot of espresso, a dash of heavy cream, one pump of vanilla syrup, and served extra hot," he said, interrupting me.

"What?" I asked, caught off by his response.

He rose, and I raised my chin to meet his gaze.

"You said you had a good memory. That's my coffee order. Don't forget to mention you quit *after* you order my drink."

He winked, and I flew out of my chair and was out the door. Fidgeting with the contents of my purse, I retrieved my car keys and slammed my palm onto the elevator button. I was only in his office for minutes and sweat covered every curve of my body, but the wet sensation in my panties blindsided me.

CHAPTER 4
F*ck Me~Aiden

I HAD to get her out of my sight before I did something I regretted. Who the fuck did she think she was walking in here with irresistible curves, a big bubble butt, and plump lips that were just waiting to be kissed. *Get your shit together, Aiden.* Even if I could have her, it would be a bad idea. For one, she's now my employee, and two, she's old enough to be my daughter. I nearly choked on the breath lodged in my lungs when I opened the door and saw her standing there. Her supple curvaceous figure, paired with those big chocolate eyes, was enough to finish me.

I needed an assistant, so I had to control my emotions and my dick. She came sauntering back in about thirty minutes later with my coffee in hand and a creamy oozing danish in the other. I didn't know why but my mouth watered just thinking about watching my cum seep out of her tight little pussy. Unsure of where to set her things, she piled her purse and danish in her lap as she sank into the chair.

She really was unqualified, and I doubt she would be helpful to me, but letting her go wasn't an option. The moment I laid eyes on her in the coffeehouse, she reeled me in. My brain fought the thoughts and urges right away, but getting her out of my head would have been a challenge. I never believed in luck, but I guess it favored me because she applied for my executive assistant position. I pulled a brand-new laptop from my desk and placed it in front of her.

"Here. You're going to need this," I said as I slid it over.

The whites of her eyes brighten as if she has never seen a brand new state-of-the-art laptop before. Having the best technology on hand was part of working in private security.

"Thanks," she said in a timid voice.

A beat of silence passed between the two of us, and then a knock sounded at the door. Eli from HR walked in, and I instructed Olivia to follow him to her desk. She followed close behind, nearly dropping her danish on the floor. Once seated, Eli pulled out his tablet and started on his long and drawn-out boring onboarding process. He gave her the rundown, provided her with the form to fill out for her badge, and got her all settled in.

I wanted to tell him all of that wasn't needed. Her task would be simple, with most of her day focused on my email and schedule. I kept my eyes on her as long as I could before the sound of my phone broke my trance.

Prying my eyes from her luscious figure would be a losing challenge. I eyed her every movement, counting under my breath the many times she tucked her chestnut locks behind her ear or pressed her bee-stung lips together as her brain went to work. She had no idea she made my cock a raging beast in my pants and waiting for her to finish the onboarding process was a grueling experience. She finally finished and rose to her feet. Witnessing her gear up before coming back into my office was the cutest fucking thing. I loved that she couldn't see me peeking through the crack of my door.

"Hi," she said as she placed a soft knock on the door.

Her syrupy sweet voice—agony. *What the fuck, Aiden.* I clenched my jaw and crooked a finger for her to enter. I avoided women for the past six years, and their seductive advances never impacted me, but Olivia was chipping away at my wall, and she had no idea just how dangerous doing so was.

I rounded my desk until we were standing a few inches from each other. "I need my calendar organized..." I let my words trail off as I sliced my eyes back to my computer.

She took that as her cue and walked behind my desk.

"Sit," I demanded.

I followed her and stood behind her in my chair. Her scent was intoxicating. Fuck, everything about her was intoxicating. My cock stirred at her clumsiness. Did I make her nervous? I pressed into the back of my chair, purposely looming over as I focused on her actions. For someone who had zero experience in administrative work, she knew how to organize a calendar pretty damn well.

She tilted her head back, exposing her neck as she looked up at me. "Um, do you want important reminders sent to your phone?"

Those eyes, those big brown eyes. My mouth watered, and the longer she held our gaze, the deeper the crack in my wall became. I nodded, and she returned her attention to the screen. She continued clicking away, and I lowered my nose to the crown of her head, inhaling the sweet scent of her shampoo. Tempted by the slit in her blouse, I clasped my hands behind my back, or my fingers would have become tangled in her soft tresses while my other hand teased her pebbled nipples.

I raised my head and faced the window. Biting back on my molars as I stared out into the skyline, I tried to reason with myself, but I promised that I wouldn't get my heart involved in another relationship, love was no longer in the cards for me. The only thing that deserved my attention was my security firm. I needed to forget about her, but now that she was my assistant, I knew that would be an uphill battle.

"Okay, I'm all done. Anything else?"

Refusing to meet her gaze, I kept my back to her. "Go down to the copy center, and pick up the bundles of training material for the three new hires."

"Okay, umm, where is the copy center." Fuck, her voice was going to be the death of me.

I shoved my hands in my pockets and shifted. "Take the elevators to the lower level and follow the signs for the copy center. Can you do that?"

"Sure."

"Good girl." *Fuck.*

A beat of silence passed between us, and I racked my brain on how to remedy the situation. Focusing on the skyline, her curvy figure came into my peripheral vision.

"Um, do I need a badge or something? I don't have mine yet."

"Take mine. It's next to the keyboard."

She grabbed my badge and walked out the door. I released the breath lodged in my throat and shifted my now very erect cock. The words slipped off my tongue before I could force them back down, and the worst part about it was how good those fucking words tasted. She was a good girl, that was apparent, but she was also hiding something. I've kept a running tally on how many times her phone chimed throughout the brief time we'd spent together.

Consistent text messages and missed calls. I owned one of the top security firms in Stonebridge, and even my phone didn't disrupt me every ten minutes. It was concerning; hell, I was concerned. I needed to know who was blowing up her phone and why. I waited a few minutes after she left and then made my way to her desk. Her scent assaulted me when I walked up to her desk, and fuck, did I want to eat her.

I found her small mint green purse sitting on the edge of the desk, and my mouth watered at the sight of it. I never liked going through other people's items, but getting my hands on something that belonged to Olivia made my flesh tingle. I unclasped the latch and peeked inside. A small wallet, a tube of lip gloss, and her keys greeted me, but no phone. I wondered if she had taken it with her, but then a loud vibration sounded from inside one of the drawers. *Bingo.*

Her phone vibrated again, and a text message slid across the screen. With her unlocked phone in my hand, I pressed on the messenger icon that revealed a string of concerning messages from numerous numbers she didn't have saved on her phone. I didn't have to run the numbers to know they were from a burner phone, but my need to know who the fuck kept texting her grew immensely.

The elevator sounded, and I made my way back to my desk. Taking a sip of my now cooled coffee, she returned to my office with a stack of neatly organized papers, only for them to become a mess below her eyes as she stepped out of her flat. I rose to my feet, rounding my desk, and she lowered to her knees at that exact moment. I should have stayed seated, but my legs disobeyed me, and I found myself standing in front of her.

Her eyes lifted, and I realized just how much I loved seeing her in this position. I reached out my hand, and my blood turned to lava. She flinched and retreated as she tried to make herself smaller. I took a step back and shoved my fist into my pockets. Her big brown eyes were now filled with fear, and I had a bone to pick with the piece of shit guy who was responsible for hurting her.

CHAPTER 5
The Next Day ~ Olivia

I WAITED in my car for a few minutes before going in. Yesterday ended in a complete bust. Or that's what I thought. I scooped up the papers and shuffled them into a semi neat pile on his desk. He didn't say a word, but he didn't have to because his face said enough. With his hands balled into fists, and his voice low, he dismissed me for the rest of the day and told me to come back in the morning. I offered to fix the order of the papers, but he held up his hand in protest.

I chalked it up to him being upset at my clumsiness and walked out. Exhausted and hungry, I made my way to my favorite taco joint, then made a pit stop at Fur Baby Delight for Oreo's special treat. Mia reassured me that he would forget all about it, but how could he forget about me falling flat on my face and messing up his documents. The alarm on my phone blared, knocking me out of my 15-minute daydream, and I killed the engine.

Trying to go unnoticed, I made my way to my desk when his office door swung open, and two men walked out. Settling into my chair, I powered on the computer and glanced at his calendar. His schedule was normally filled with daily outings and numerous meetings over zoom, but today stood out like a sore thumb because he had nothing scheduled. My phone buzzed, and I pressed the decline button. It wasn't even 10 a.m. and that was the twentieth missed call from Damien. Setting my phone back on the desk, it buzzed again, and this time I didn't bother hitting the declined button.

Squeezing my phone in my hand, I hurried down the hall in the hopes I would be out of earshot from Aiden. Once the line clicked over, Damien started his groveling, a river of empty promises and lots of lies. I pleaded with him to stop calling, only for his voice to raise in anger and for him to call me every degrading name he could think of. I closed my eyes to fight back the tears and jabbed my finger on the end call button.

Mia urged me to change my number because blocking him wasn't enough. No matter how many numbers I blocked, he would call from another. My stomach grumbled, reminding me that I hadn't had my breakfast, and begged me to eat something. I started back toward my desk but took a quick glance into his office. Unaware that he could see me through the crack, our eyes met, and I shot my eyes to the floor. *You're an idiot, Olivia.*

"Olivia..." The timbre in his voice made the hairs on the back of my neck stand as my name rolled off his tongue. So smooth, so dark.

I sauntered inside and tucked a lock of hair behind my ear. He sat relaxed in his chair, with his legs spread wide and the top button of his dress shirt unbuttoned. I didn't take note of his cologne yesterday, but today it wrapped around my lungs like a snake as I inhaled. It reminded me of wood, with a hint of sage.

I clasped my hands in front of my skirt and found his gaze. "Yes."

"Are you free for the next two days?" He rested his elbow on the arm of his chair and traced the pad of his thumb over his lip.

I racked my brain and chewed the inside of my cheek as I contemplated. "I believe so. Why?"

"Good. Then you won't mind joining me on my little business trip."

"Oh, um...well..." My words turned to mush as I tried to form a coherent sentence.

He swiveled in his chair and faced the window. "Is there a problem?"

"My cat, Oreo. It's fine. I can find a sitter for her." I swallowed and picked at my cuticles as I waited for his response.

With his attention still fixated on the skyline, my flesh tingled when he jutted his jaw in my direction, and the corner of his mouth lifted.

"Turn, and stand in the corner," he commanded.

I froze, unsure of what to do, and then he repeated his words. I turned and walked to the corner. In an attempt to keep my heart from busting out of my chest, I rested one hand across my chest to give me comfort. Silence draped the office.

The leather of his chair squeaked underneath him as he stood, and the hairs on the back of my neck took notice. My mouth turned dry, and my pulse staggered. The breath lodged in my throat pushed past my lips when he placed a hand on my shoulder. Then goose bumps scattered across my skin when his soft lips found the shell of my ear. Conflict, fear, and curiosity pulled at me.

"Have you been a bad girl?" he whispered in my ear.

I shook my head, and his slow barbed laughter oozed into my ear. A wave of heat curled down my spine and landed right between my legs. How could I be confused yet turned on at the same time?

"Are you sure about that? I beg to differ." His hands slithered down to my waist, and he wrapped his muscular arms around me.

It was an odd feeling, an unfamiliar one, but it evoked a sense of safety.

I leaned into his hard chest. "I'm not a bad girl. I'm a good girl."

His grip tightened, and he pressed into me. I gasped as I felt the hardness of his erection jabbing into me.

"Oh, you'll definitely be daddy's good little girl once I'm done with you, but right now, your a naughty girl, and naughty girls stand in corners."

His python grip loosened, and the heat of his body evaporated as he stepped away and walked toward his desk. I wanted to steal a glance as he continued to work, but I couldn't. Staying as still as a statue, I made the wooden oak wall my muse as I burned with humiliation. I liked the surge of electricity that rippled down my spine when I uttered those forbidden words. *Good girl.*

It made my mouth water and had me aching in places it shouldn't. After my ten-minute punishment ended, he dismissed me. I remained in the corner for a few extra seconds to process what just happened, and then quietly rushed back to my desk. He followed my movements, his gaze unyielding as he watched me fidget with my computer.

It wasn't until an incoming call came through that I was able to release the breath I was holding in a wave of relief. With his attention on the call, I sat back, taking note of the goose bumps that lined my arms. I didn't know what possessed him to put me in a corner, but I liked it, a lot. I continued with my daily work. I learned his schedule pretty quickly. He took his lunches from 12:30 p.m. to 1:00 p.m. and needed a coffee refill around 2:00 p.m. He spent the end of the day with his security force, which put me in charge of all incoming calls and emails until he returned.

Luckily the notes attached to his hectic calendar provided me with the answers for the few calls that did come in. The day flew by, and in the blink of an eye, the clock read 5:30 p.m. I shut down my laptop and shoved it into my bag. Hoping to sneak out without being noticed, I attempted to speed walk to the elevators when his call stopped me in my tracks.

"Be ready tonight," he said as he kept his stare locked on the screen in front of him.

"Tonight? I thought the convention wasn't until Wednesday?"

The unexpected vibration of my phone made me jump, and I shifted through my purse as I kept my eyes on him.

He plucked at the cuff of his shirt before lowering the screen of his laptop. "It is." He stood and rounded the corner of his desk until he stopped mere inches from me. "But I want to get there the night before. So be ready by 9 p.m. I'll have my car pick you up."

CHAPTER 6
Peep Show ~ Aiden

I KEPT my eyes on her delectable ass as she disappeared down the hall. I never attended conventions on the first day because I hated big crowds, but I needed Olivia all to myself. I fought with my limbs the entire time she stood in my doorway. I wanted to bend her over my desk, fuck her sweet little cunt and then tell her how fucking beautiful she was, but I held off. She carried a mountain of pain in her heart, and I wanted to be the one to soothe her broken spirit because seeing her hurt was too much to bear.

Making her stand in the corner was a risk, but it was one that I was willing to take, earning her trust was the biggest obstacle I'd have to overcome. It didn't take a rocket scientist to figure out she just got out of an abusive relationship. From the moment she stepped foot in the office this morning, her phone fired off every twenty minutes. She finally snatched it and walked to the other end of the long hallway where the kitchenette and fridges were located. I followed her and leaned against a wall within earshot.

The desperation in her voice made my chest tighten with pain. I had no intentions of bringing her to the convention, but I couldn't sleep at night knowing she was all alone with that piece of shit harassing her. I texted Jasper and told him I would rather go alone, and he didn't fight me on it. *How dare that piece of shit human threaten my baby girl.*

Forcing her to pack her bags at the drop of a hat wasn't ideal, but she left me no choice. I finished up the rest of my work and closed up my office. The ride back to my condo was swift, and I alerted my housekeeper earlier in the day that I'd be leaving town. Once home, it took less than an hour to pack, leaving me with time to spare, and I knew exactly where I wanted to spend it.

My driver headed toward South Shore, Stonebridge's less appealing neighborhood. For the most part, the town of Stonebridge was picturesque in every way, except for where Olivia lived. I eyed the littered streets and demolished buildings as my car zoomed by. A group of men occupying a corner turned their heads in the car's direction as we slowed, and it ground my gears that she had so little safety surrounding her. My car pulled up to her block and stopped in front of a building that looked like what nightmares were made of.

I spotted an abandoned rundown parking lot across the street and told my driver to move over there. Olivia lived in a two-story building, and from the looks of it, the window with the pink curtains and the cat nestled on the windowsill had to be hers. Apart of me felt like a creep for peering into her window as I waited for her to get ready, but then again, her safety was at stake, and who was I to ignore my sweet baby girl who was in trouble.

I got out of the car and perched my ass on the hood, binoculars in hand. She was so fucking cute, the way she trotted around in her purple bra and panties. She had no idea just how transparent her little curtains were. This is why I couldn't let her go; she was too vulnerable. I've been battling with my emotions for the past 24 hours, and no matter what excuse I came up with against pursuing her, none of them were good enough. After six whole years of being alone, she's the one who broke my spell. I didn't bother telling Jasper because he would either call me crazy or chalk it up to me being horny and wanting a good fuck.

She disappeared into another room, and her cat stayed planted on the windowsill. Her street was almost pitch black due to the row of broken streetlights. She returned a few minutes later, holding a clear bowl of colorful cereal. She scooped a spoonful in her mouth and continued shoving items into what I believed was a suitcase of some sort. A cream-colored car pulled up behind her little hatchback, and a girl with long dark hair powered up the steps.

I relaxed my posture and slid my thumb across my bottom lip. The same girl appeared in her bedroom a few seconds later and grabbed the cat off the windowsill. They talked for a few minutes, and I focused on Olivia's reactions. Her arms flung out to her side, and a smile bigger than Texas spread across her face as she showed the girl something I couldn't quite make out. Witnessing her innocent actions made a tingle crawl down my spine. I folded my arms across my chest and let a lazy smirk spread across my lips.

Soon, I watched as her friend loaded the cat carrier into the backseat and then climbed into the driver's side of her vehicle. My attention sliced back to the window, and Olivia slipped on a t-shirt and jeans. She finished off her bowl of cereal by shoving two scoops past her lips as she walked out of her bedroom. My spine stiffened when a dark-colored car pulled up in front of her apartment. Being in the military, I learned the hard way to never ignore my gut, and my gut was telling me the car that just pulled up was trouble.

I signaled to my driver to kill the engine and told him to pop the trunk. I retrieved a switchblade from the inside pocket of my leather duffle and slid it into my back pocket before returning to the front of the car.

The driver's door opened, and a man climbed out. I could have kicked myself for not looking up her piece of a shit ex-boyfriend. The man paced back and forth, raking his hands through his hair as he looked up at Olivia's window.

I had a good hunch that this man was Olivia's ex, and my blood boiled. The darkness that surrounded me concealed my identity, and once my hand landed on his shoulder, I swung him around and slammed his back into the brick wall of the apartment building.

"Looking for someone?" I spat.

He fought my resistance and attempted to reach in his pocket, but my forearm, conveniently resting on his windpipe, halted his movements. I knew guys like him. Guys who believed they were the best fucking thing since sliced bread and thought women were their personal punching bags.

He struggled against my hold. "Who the fuck are you?"

I eased in and let the corner of my mouth lift. "Your worst fucking nightmare."

He struggled to breathe as his body started to tremble in my hold. I could have easily ended his life, and no one would know, but I wasn't that man anymore. Still, making sure this asshole understood that he would be signing his death certificate if he ever contacted Olivia again didn't escape me.

"A scar would look real nice down the side of your

face." I placed the cool steel to his cheek, and he whimpered. I enjoyed his constant struggle.

I opted to forgo the knife and made sure he felt the throbbing ache of my fist. Each blow was harder than the next, and I ensured he got the fucking message. He slithered to the ground like a broken doll, and a river of blood coagulated around his nose and lips. Unable to speak, he held out his hand in a plea, and I kneeled.

"Call Olivia again, and I promise you that'll be the last call you make."

I left him to ponder my promise and reached for my phone.

Aiden: My car is downstairs

Baby Girl: K

CHAPTER 7
First Kiss ~ Olivia

AIDEN TEXTED me right when I was going to warm up some ramen noodles. My small bowl of cereal wasn't enough to curb my hunger, and I hadn't had any real food all day. I pulled my suitcase off my bed and rolled it near the door. Doing a double check to make sure all the lights were off, I grabbed my purse and headed down the stairs. The convention was only two days, so I didn't need that many clothes, well that's what I told myself as I hauled my large suitcase with a week's worth of clothing down the stairs.

A luxury sedan with midnight tinted windows idled outside the door with Aiden leaning against it. A fitted t-shirt concealed his muscular frame, and a pair of dark denim jeans stretched over his trunk-like legs. I didn't know if it was the carnal stare in his eyes or the sudden chill running down my spine from the wind, but my grasp weakened, and my suitcase toppled to the bottom of the steps.

Beating me to it, he scooped down and grabbed the handle of my suitcase with one hand as he pulled me into his embrace with the other. I inhaled him and forced his masculine scent around my lungs. My pulse turned into a thundering stampede, and his forehead found mine. I shouldn't want this. Aiden was old enough to be my dad, and I told myself I would take a break from relationships, but this was different. Aiden was different.

His grip around my waist tightened, and his fingers found their rightful place tangled within my tresses. "Promise not to pull away, okay?"

Before I could answer, his lips came crashing down on mine and ruined me. Time stilled, my pulse mellowed, and a cloud of safety swallowed me for the first time in a long time. He held me tight with lips locked as his fingers caressed my scalp. The sound of the driver slamming the trunk shut broke our trance, and Aiden stepped aside. I brushed the loose hair strands out of my face and ran a hand down my shirt as I slid into the vehicle.

The inside of the car smelled just like him, and a wave of tingles skittered down my spine. Settling in the seat, I leaned back and waited for Aiden to slide in. I teased my tongue over my lips, eager to consume the leftover taste of our kiss. He sat close to me and placed his hand on my thigh, giving me a light squeeze. With questions about our trip on the tip of my tongue, they dissolved when I caught a glimpse of the cracked skin on his knuckles.

I brushed my fingers over it and lifted my eyes to meet his gaze. "What happened to your hand?"

He lifted it and flexed his fingers a few times. "Ah, nothing. I just had to teach some asshat a fucking lesson. I'll ice it on the plane." Tiny dots of blood bubbled to the surface as he flexed once more before lowering his hand back down to my thigh. With the taste of his kiss still on my lips, my mind raced as I digested just how good it felt, how safe it felt. He kissed me like he's known me for years and held me like he never wanted to let go. He kept his hand on my thigh as he powered through a few emails on his phone, and I texted Mia everything she needed to know so Oreo would be comfortable. The car slowed, and we pulled up next to a private jet.

"You have a jet?" My words came out fast, and I placed my hand over my mouth in embarrassment.

He smiled and climbed out of the car. "No, but I like to rent them whenever I travel. Not a fan of the hassle of commercial flying, plus we needed to be alone, there is only the two pilots, no flight crew."

Alone? His words made me sizzle, and a pool of saliva blanketed my mouth. He held out his hand, and I grabbed it. The lights from the jet lit up the surrounding area, making my heart thump in my chest as I climbed the steps. I've never flown in a private plane before; hell, I never even flown first class. The strong scent of vanilla slapped me in the face as I boarded. Plush, cream-colored chairs outlined with marbleized wood were scattered throughout. I walked cautiously down the aisle, stopping at the chair with the cream soda and grilled cheese sitting on the tray table.

"That's for you," Aiden said as he closed in on me.

He held out his hand, instructing me to sit. I sank into the plush seat and nestled my head against the headrest. I looked around, taking in the decor, the lights, and everything else. Aiden joined me, taking the seat across from me. I stretched my legs and looked around once more. The amount of space provided from the seat and the aisle aided in shoving all my insecurities to the side. For the first time, I didn't have to make myself smaller just to make someone else feel comfortable. I relaxed my arms and let them fall to my side. The seam of his mouth torn into a small smile, and he winged a brow.

Every time he did that, butterflies swarmed in my belly, but I wasn't going to tell him. I kicked my feet out and swung them around. Although he was sitting across from me, there was well over two feet between us. He adjusted in his seat and let his long legs spread apart. My eyes landed on his crotch, and when I looked up, his eyes were locked on mine.

A wave of heat rushed to my cheeks, and I snatched the grilled cheese off the plate next to me. Pushing the warm bread past my lips, I savored the gooey goodness of melted cheese and roasted tomato. I kept my eyes down, my legs crossed, and lips sealed as I devoured the sandwich.

"How did you know I liked grilled cheese?" I wiped the crumbs from my mouth and swallowed down the last bite.

The corners of his eyes creased. "I had a hunch." He winked and placed his elbow on the armrest as he slid his thumb across his bottom lip.

I ignored his gesture and pulled my cream soda out of the holder. The straw bobbed, and I pinched two fingers around it to hold it in place. I didn't know where to look. Looking around was obvious, and looking him in the eye just made me ache in places that chilled me to the bone. I found the safety of the floor and rested my eyes on the dark carpet as I finished my drink. I placed the empty soda bottle back in the holder and leaned back in my seat. Still fixated on me, his gaze made me feel like prey, but it didn't make me want to run away. The sound of the hatch slamming shut made me jump, and the plane went dark. Silence draped us, with only the engine's howl sputtering to life.

I guess he could feel the thickness in the air from my anxiety because his hand found mine. My back clung to the seat as we took off, and I closed my eyes, counting back from ten as I prayed for my grilled cheese to stay in my stomach. Once the plane leveled out, the lights turned on but dimmed to a warm hue, and Aiden didn't let go of my hand either. It was an odd feeling. Just the two of us, alone. With his fingers still intertwined with mine, he leaned back in his seat and tugged.

"Aiden...?" I let my words trail off.

The strength of his pull was unyielding, and by the time he let go of my hand, I was situated between his legs and on my knees. I couldn't even fight the fact that I felt comfortable in this position. Being so close to him, with his legs like steel bars enclosing me, broke down my walls. He tucked his finger under my chin, demanding my attention, and eased in until his warm breath tickled the shell of my ear.

"Are you my good girl?"

I nodded and let my butt sink further to the ground.

He growled, and placed my hands on his muscular thighs. "Good, because daddy's got a hard dick, and it's begging for a release.

A sudden flush of warmth spread through me at his words, exuding a sense of dominance and protection, something I craved for so long. The raspy sound of his zipper coming undone filled the air, and then his monstrous manhood sprung forward. Its swollen tip dripped a clear fluid, and I embarrassingly licked my bottom lip.

He told me to take off my top, and I hesitated but eventually did as instructed. The last man I got undressed in front of was Damien, and he made sure to berate me about my size every time. I soon became numb to his cruel words as I let them flow in one ear and out the other, but he still succeeded in stripping away a layer of my self-esteem with the whip of his tongue.

"Bra..."

The deep timbre in his voice made my mouth water, and I let the straps of my bra fall down my shoulders. Exposed, with bare breasts and pebbled nipples, he fixated. My arms found a comfortable position in front of my stomach, and he touched my arm, forcing them away.

CHAPTER 8
Just a Taste ~ Aiden

I FINALLY HAD Olivia where I wanted her, or I hoped so. Taking things slow wasn't an option with her. The last thing I wanted to do was push her away. I craved her trust more than anything, but my cock refused to lay dormant in my pants. We had a 3-hour flight, and I booked a private charter for a reason, and it had everything to do with having her all alone. I loved the way she tried to hide her luscious curves from me.

Nothing about her fit into normalized beauty standards. She had medium-length chestnut hair that outlined her heart-shaped face, a soft belly that could double as a pillow, one I'll happily lay on, and thighs thicker than freshly raised dough. The button nose in the middle of her face was the icing on the cake. I was dying for a taste, and the walls of my mouth filled with saliva as my cock leaked at the tip.

"You look so fucking good on your knees, baby girl," I said as I stroked my flesh.

Her cheeks turned a shade darker, and a low hum vibrated off my lips. I had one goal; to gain her trust and make her feel like the most beautiful girl in the world. The cold air from the vents hardened her delectable nipples, making a throb shoot down my shaft.

I lifted her chin with my index finger and instructed her to stand. She paused for a moment and then rose to her feet. I fidgeted with the button next to me until the slow rhythmic beats of R&B seeped out of the speakers above.

She clasped her hands in front of her and turned her left foot inward. "I'm not good at this." Her chin lowered to her chest, and her eyes met the floor.

"Now, your jeans."

I took a sip of my water as I waited for her to remove the last bit of her clothing. I followed her movements, eager to show her just how crazy she made me.

"Close your eyes, and dance for daddy. Don't think, just dance."

She pulled her bottom lip between her teeth and slowly closed her eyes. I increased the music volume just enough to make her feel like she was all alone, but not loud enough that it would drown out my moans as I stroked to her movements. I wanted her to hear what she did to me, how she made my dick leak like a broken faucet. She finally yielded to the music, and her fingers traveled up and down her body in a slow intoxicating motion.

With each moan that pushed past my lips, her fingers teased her suckable nipples as her hips moved. I wanted to blow my load when she eased her head back as her hands slid down her body. I lifted my hand, now sticky with my sap, and tugged at her arm. I pulled her forward and then turned her around, forcing her ass to my face.

"Sit on daddy's lap."

I placed my hands on her hips and forced her onto my lap. She stilled her movements for a few seconds as she absorbed the violent throb of my cock, and then she did exactly what I wanted her to. She rocked. Her hips moved back and forth in a slow circular motion, and the sensation of her lace panties against my shaft stirred a tingle in the base of my spine. I got a hold of her pebbled nipples and pinched them between my fingers. *Fuck.* A whimper of pleasure dripped off her lips, and she rocked harder.

I pinched harder before twisting them, and a sharp moan pushed past her lips. The edge of my mouth morphed into a smile, and I pressed my lips to her soft back. At this point, the soft music was no match for the sounds dripping off our lips, and I wrapped my arms around her soft waist as my teeth dug into the tenderness of her shoulder. The rocking stopped once she registered the jerk of my body, and I let out a low drawn out-groan.

With the crotch of her panties soaked in my seed, she stood, but before she could turn around, I tucked my thumb under the waistband and pulled them down to her ankles.

"Does baby girl have a wet little cunt now?" I asked as I waited for her to step out of her panties.

She nodded and stood before me naked. She had no idea how fucking perfect she was, and I would make it my life mission that she knew it every damn day.

I balled up her panties and forced them into my back pocket. "Good, because daddy's going to make you my little slut for the next two days."

ONCE SHE REDRESSED, I cradled her in my arms the rest of the flight, and she dozed off. The abrupt halt of the plane slamming onto the runway woke her from her nap, and I placed a small kiss on her forehead. With sleepy eyes and a yawn teetering on the edge of her lips, she pressed her fingers to my chest and lifted. The lights in the distance caught her attention, and she fixed on them like a cat discovering wool for the first time. Surprisingly she never asked me where the convention was being held. The whites of her eyes brightened as the jet made its way down the runway.

"Are you excited, sweetie?" I asked as I ran a knuckle down her soft cheek.

The latch opened, and Olivia hopped down the steps with excitement flowing through her bones. *So fucking cute.* I wondered if she had ever been to a resort like this one before; from the look on her face, I doubted it, which made my heart bloom. I guided her through the airport, taking her hand in mine, and steered her toward the exit where a black sedan waited for us.

"I thought this was a security convention?" She slid into the car and swung her legs in front of her as she stared out the window.

I slid in beside her and wedged my arm between her back and the leather seat. "Well, it's better to chat with like-minded people over a beautiful sunset than in a dull conference room."

She smiled and tapped the toes of her tennis shoes together as she swung her legs. It nearly killed me. I forgot that the annual private security conference took place here. I've had the luxury of traveling all over the world more times than I could count, so being here didn't have the same effect on me that it did, Olivia. The car pulled into the circle of our hotel, and I grabbed her hand. I needed to hold on to her to keep her safe and to prevent her from running off due to excitement. I tugged her arm and swung her body in front of mine as we approached the front desk. Resting my chin on the top of her head, she toyed with the colorful pamphlets in the display holder as I checked us in.

"Good evening, Mr. West. I see we have you in the two-bedroom—"

"Can you switch that out for your one-bedroom executive suite?"

I no longer needed the two-bedroom suite. There was no way in hell my baby girl was sleeping in a separate room, let alone a separate bed from mine. I pressed my front into Olivia's back, giving her a sneak peek at the monster begging to be let out. She took notice and lifted her chin to the ceiling until her intoxicating eyes met mine. I grabbed the keycards and pulled Olivia toward the elevators. It seemed like time came to a brutal crawl once the jet landed. I needed Olivia in my bed, and I needed her there now.

CHAPTER 9
His Good Girl~Olivia

THE RESORT WAS like nothing I'd ever seen, but I never had the luxury of globe-trotting. My worldly travels included a yearly visit down south to visit my aunt and a trip to Cancun in college. The elevator doors peeled back, and we walked inside a glass dome. My stomach dropped as it whisked us up to the very top level. Trading marble title for plush decorative carpet, Aiden swiped the keycard on the door reader, and my breath caught in my throat. The view had me running to the balcony. I'd only seen these types of places on TV, and for the first time in my life, I felt like I was living a dream rather than a nightmare that refused to end.

Calm waves swayed below the limitless midnight sky, and a gust of warm wind crashed against my body. I tilted my head as I absorbed the tranquility of my surroundings. Aiden pulled me into his grasp and dragged me back inside. I wanted to stay up and explore the amenities, but the yawn that escaped my lips let me know my body had other plans. He picked me up, carrying me to the bedroom where a king-size bed drenched in the softest cotton I'd ever seen teased me.

"Time for bed, baby." He gave me a gentle spank on my butt as he shoved me toward the bathroom.

I protested and folded my arms across my chest. "I'm too old for bedtimes," I spat.

"You might be too old for bedtimes, but you're not too old for me to show you what I'll do if you don't fix that little bratty attitude."

He winged a brow and took another step closer and then another until he forced me into the bathroom. A modern purple claw foot tub sat in the middle, surrounded by a matching vanity that spanned from one side of the wall to the next. He didn't take no as an answer and turned the gold knobs of the tub until a wave of hot water splashed down from the faucet. Every time he moved, my eyes fixated on his hard body. The man was made of muscle, and seeing the tiny veins trapped below the skin of his arms flex with each movement made my knees turn to water.

He wasted no time grabbing the luxury toiletries off the vanity and pouring them into the raging water.

Not caring about using every ounce for one bath, he emptied the entire medium size bottle of bubble bath before chucking it in the trash. A cloud of honey and vanilla masked the air, and I closed my eyes and took a deep breath. My quick trance of tranquility was interrupted by the force of his chest against mine, and I shot my eyes open.

"Ready?" he asked as he pulled a loose strand of hair out of my face.

I nodded and took a step back. Slicing my eyes to the tub and then at the door, he placed his hands on his hips and waited.

"Um, are you going to watch me take a bath?" I stepped out of my jeans and then pulled my top over my head.

"Absolutely not. Daddy's going to bathe you and then put you to bed." He traced his thumb over his bottom lip and waited. *Damn, this man had patience.*

My shoulders tensed at his response, maybe because I had never had anyone bathe me before. I pushed my thoughts out of my head and unclasped my bra. It floated to the floor, and Aiden's eyes landed on my breasts. Once naked, he took my hand and guided me to the tub. He dipped his hand in and then whisked the excess water from his hand before picking me up. I yelped at the gesture, and he gently lowered me into the tub. The warm water calmed my pulse, relaxing my muscles as it enveloped me.

Snatching the sponge off the counter, he plunged it into the warm water and pressed it against my thighs.

He had a carnal look in his eyes, which reminded me of a predator. He pressed down a little harder, and I separated my legs, just like he wanted. A small part of my brain tried to fight this unusual dynamic. I always had to be the adult in every relationship I endured.

I was always left to carry the weight and often left to pick up the pieces after it all went to shit, but with Aiden, there was nothing I had to carry, no boulder to weigh me down. He consumed me, gave me praise, and put every inch of my body and mind on a pedestal. I couldn't deny the comfort that absorbed me when he called me baby girl or the way my pussy wept when he called me his little slut.

He dragged the sponge between my thighs and up my stomach. "That's it. Be a good girl and relax for daddy."

With his arm elbow-deep in the bubbles, the water whooshed around my breasts and turned my nipples hard. He washed every inch of my body, paying extra attention to the leftover bruise on my right shoulder, and then rose to his feet. He grabbed the clear bottle of shampoo and popped the top. Pouring more than a dime-size amount, the clear liquid ran off the edge of his palm and down his arm.

His fingers found my wet tresses, and he pulled

my head back, forcing my eyes to meet his. As the cool liquid dissolved into my scalp, I closed my eyes and exhaled a breath when his fingers dug into my scalp.

His lips grazed the shell of my ear, and his words seeped in like a lazy river. "Tell daddy what you are."

My mouth parted, with syllables lining up to answer his question, but the only audible response I gave was a faint moan as his fingers pinched my left nipple. His lips found my other ear, and he asked once more. This time, he didn't hold back the bass in his voice.

"I'm daddy's little slut." I turned my head slightly, just enough to see the corner of his mouth curl into a devilish smile.

He jerked my head back with a light tug. "My little cum slut. Daddy's going to use your mouth tonight, tomorrow, and every damn day after that." He walked around the tub and released the plug.

The water whirled as it charged down the drain, and Aiden stretched out his hand. Before the first shiver could wash over me, he wrapped me in a large plush towel and led me to the bed. Not letting a minute go past so I could dry off, he snatched the towel from my damp body, and an army of goose bumps covered it once the cold air from the vents swept past me.

Toeing out of his loafers, he removed his shirt, jeans, and boxers. His flesh dripped at the tip and looked angrier than when he whipped it out last. I wondered if his well ever dried. He didn't need to command me to drop down to my knees; I did it on my own. The more he kept me in his sphere; the more my body reacted to his gestures. It craved positive reinforcement, and Aiden gave me just that. He rewarded me with praise and kindness, so I happily obliged.

"Look at you. So fucking beautiful on your knees, and I didn't even have to ask you. You want a reward, don't you?"

I sat back on my ankles, with my hands on my thighs and my chin lifted. He positioned his cock a few inches from my mouth and let his precum drop onto the bow of my lips. The feeling sent electricity through my veins as I waited patiently for his instructions.

"Open." He rested a finger under my chin and lifted my head. "Wider…"

I did as told, and his flesh plunged into the depths of my mouth. His girth stretched my jaws, and a light sting exuded from the corners of my mouth at the intrusion.

"That's my girl; look at you warming daddy's cock in your little mouth. Such a good girl."

He threaded his fingers through my wet tresses until they were tangled between the slits of his fingers. Holding my head in place, he retrieved his cock from my mouth and then plunged it back in before I could take a breath. The corners of his eyes creased, and low grunts dripped off his lips as he fucked my mouth. Our gaze never broke, but once he slowed his motions, I braced myself for the thick rope of semen.

The palms of his hands rested on my cheeks as he emptied himself in my mouth. Unable to swallow it all down in one go, some of it seeped out and trailed down my chin. His eyes crinkled with a smile, and he pulled back. Admiring me for a few seconds before he wiped my mouth, he gestured me to stand. Rising to my feet, he pulled me into his chest and kissed my forehead softly.

"Daddy's so fucking proud of you."

CHAPTER 10
Hate Me ~ Aiden

ONCE I TOOK HER MOUTH, I cleaned her up and carried her to bed. Since she was such a good girl, I rewarded her with a late-night snack. A few warm chocolate chip cookies and a glass of warm milk. A permanent smile stained her lips as she ate each one, and it was the cutest thing I had ever seen. I waited for her to finish and swiped my thumb across the corners of her mouth to remove the leftover crumbs. It didn't take her long to doze off once the warm milk hit her system and her eyelids fell heavy. Streams of sunlight seeped through the blinds, and I ran my hands through Olivia's soft tresses. Sleep wasn't in the cards for me last night, mainly because I couldn't keep my eyes off Olivia.

Although she was in the safety of my grasp, her past still haunted her dreams. She tossed and turned as words I couldn't quite make out dripped off her tongue. It killed me to see her struggle to sleep. I tried to console her, but my light touches made her flinch every time, and it nearly broke me in half.

I regretted not telling her what I did to her ex-boyfriend, and maybe I should have when she asked what happened to my hands. Eventually, a wave of exhaustion forced my eyes shut, but not for long. Sunlight seeped into the room from the balcony straining my eyes open. My phone chimed, alerting me that the convention would be starting soon.

A part of me wished I had made Jasper join me, because I could have pawned him off to do all my bidding and stayed with Olivia all day. A cute moan echoed off her lips, and she turned, placing her butt right into my crotch. My cock took notice, and I fought the urge to stick the tip in her tight little hole.

She needed rest, good rest. I kissed her cheek and winced as I removed myself from the warm bed. Slipping into the shower, I palmed my cock and went to work, jerking myself off to thoughts of her. Biting back on my molars, I controlled the grunts that begged to push past my lips and slammed my hand into the cool tile.

Once I imagined her back on her knees, with my cock between her lips, that familiar feeling didn't take long to settle at the base of my spine. I came, and the feeling was fleeting once ribbons of my seed coated the shower floor. Jerking off wasn't ideal, and I only used it for a quick fix. The next time I released, it would be inside of Olivia, and I planned to come good and hard.

I slipped into something business casual and placed one more kiss on Olivia's shoulder before heading downstairs. The buzz from my phone stole my attention, and I pulled it out of my pocket.

Jenny: When are you coming to visit me? I miss you.

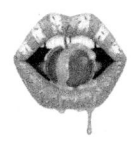

ONE THING I hated about these conventions was overly aggressive vendors. Some of them really did have a good product, but most of them were just selling cheap shit with a jacked-up price. I made my rounds, stopping every so often to engage with other owners who had private security firms. My phone chimed, and I knew Jasper was texting to ask me if I was enjoying myself. *Asshole.*

Double-checking the time on my phone, I noticed it was a little past noon and wondered about Olivia. Running back to the suite wasn't an option due to the distance, and calling her wasn't an option either since I locked her phone in the suite safe. The last thing I needed was her ex trying his hand again with empty threats. A tap on the shoulder forced me to turn, and before I could wave off the invitation, the CEO of another private security firm swept me into a conversation.

As I searched the floor, I yielded to his ramblings, and Olivia soon came into my peripheral vision. She stood out like a sore thumb in the sea of muscular frames surrounding her. I took a step back and sliced my attention to her. The CEO currently holding me hostage took the hint and patted me on the shoulder before retreating in the opposite direction. I couldn't explain it, but it was like all the light left her eyes when mine landed on hers, making my heart slow to a crawl.

"Baby girl," I said as I stepped into her sphere. She smelled divine, and I had to restrain myself from pulling her into my grasp. I clipped a finger under her chin and examined her heart-shaped face.

She cut her gaze to the side of me. "I got lost, this hotel is so big, and there are so many people. I'm shocked I found you."

"I know, baby. You could have stayed in the suite if you wanted. Did you sleep okay?" I grabbed her hand, tugging her in my direction. I still had a few more vendors to check out before taking her back to the suite and fucking her brains out like the little slut she was.

"Have you been checking your email? An important message came through, and that's why I came down. They sent one this morning also." She stretched out her hand and waited for me to take my tablet.

I could sense the strain in her voice as she spoke and paused for a second before I took it. I opened the email app and pressed on the highlighted ones. Typing quickly, I replied and switched it off before handing it back to her.

"Did you sleep, okay, baby?" I brushed a piece of hair behind her ear and observed her.

She nodded and sliced her eyes to the concrete floor. Something was obviously wrong, and as much as I wanted to know what was bothering her, seeing her turn into a little brat turned my cock hard. My hand found hers, and I pulled her along. Everything must have been overwhelming for her because it was for me, and I've been to a dozen of these conventions. Refusing to let go of her hand, I kept her close and took glances in her direction every so often.

The way she sucked her bottom lip between her teeth when she had a question pondering her brain, and the way her gaze became soft as silk when something exciting caught her attention. I continued to pull her along, and she continued to try and slip from my grip.

I finally had enough and tugged her around me

until her back met my chest. "Being a little brat?" I whispered in her ear.

"No." She deadpanned.

The fire in her voice made my dick ache with need, the need for her cunt. I pressed my crouch into her lower back, ensuring she felt it. We closed in on another vendor's table, and his merchandise interested me. I made small talk with the vendor while keeping my little brat on a tight leash. I couldn't help but chuckle at her squirms. Although she was thicker than honey and over two hundred pounds, she wasn't stronger than me. My grip around her waist was like a vice, and the more she squirmed in my arms, the tighter it became.

CHAPTER 11
Second Thoughts ~ Olivia

I WOKE this morning to find Aiden had left and headed down to the convention. He had a late breakfast sent up to the room. I had no idea how he knew what I craved, but all my favorites were laid out under a nice silver dome. I devoured the buttery eggs, crispy bacon, and sweet fruit. It had been so long since I had food that tasted this good. My daily breakfast consisted of stale cereal, burnt toast, and sometimes a danish from the café.

Aiden assured me last night that I didn't have to attend the convention and I could spend my day exploring. I took that as my cue to head to the pool and catch up on the book I was reading. A few hours passed, my skin turned a shade darker, and my inner thighs begged for aloe vera and baby powder. Although I had the entire day to myself, a small part of me wanted to check Aiden's calendar and make sure he didn't miss any important emails. It was an odd feeling, letting him use my mouth and bathe me but also being worried about his calendar. He took his phone but left his tablet on the desk in the suite. His text messages and calendar were synced to all of his devices so that he would never miss a reminder.

I slipped on a pair of dark denim jeans and a nice blouse. The weather at the resort reminded me of those perfect summer days in June, full of sunshine, low humidity, and a fresh breeze. Slipping my feet into a pair of leather-strapped sandals, I turned to grab the door handle when the chime of his tablet halted me in my tracks.

I grabbed it off the desk and unlocked it. Tapping my finger on the email app, my eyes went straight to the string of unread messages in bold. I was able to answer two of them, but the other two seemed urgent, with a sharp tone. I clicked out of the app, and the messenger app's notification button stole my attention. I usually kept my nose in his email and ignored his missed calls and messages, but his attention toward his electronic devices seemed to have tapered off since we were on a business trip. My feelings about Aiden seconds before I read the text message were a cocktail of confusion, desire, and something else I couldn't put my finger on. But, after reading the text, the only thing that flowed through me was confusion and embarrassment.

I checked the time stamp, and whoever Jenny was sent this message over 4 hours ago. Aiden hadn't replied. My mind raced, wondering if he saw it and, if he did, was he purposely not responding. Annoyed that the corners of my eyes prickled with tears, I blinked and clicked the tablet off. Stepping outside the hotel room, the cold air of the vents sent a wave of goose bumps scattering across my skin.

I made my way toward the convention, but my mind was in a fog. I never asked Aiden if he was in a relationship; now, I regret it. Maybe I wanted to believe that he wasn't, due to how he treated me, kissed me, and praised me. I followed the herd of people into the elevator and found a place in the corner near the back. A man and woman were the last to get on, and they reminded me of Aiden and me, and a thought that never occurred to me before popped into my head. Was I just another notch in his belt? Another secretary to woo with luxury, fuck, and then dump.

The elevator chimed, and we all filed out. The hotel's lower level was littered with bodies as I had imagined. I followed the signs for the convention and walked through the canopy of masculine cologne that lingered in the air. One thing about Aiden, he stood out. His towering height, paired with his muscular frame, and sleek steel gray hair, made him an easy target. After ten minutes of walking in what felt like an endless circle, I spotted Aiden chatting with a man. I started toward him and then slowed as my emotions went haywire.

I shifted to the side, but it was too late, my figure had already caught his eye, and he turned. I tried my best to keep my responses clipped, but somehow my hand ended up in his, and now he had me captured in his strong, hulk-like arms.

"Ollie..." he whispered in my ear, and the hairs on the back of my neck stood.

His words caught me off guard, and heat crept under my skin. *Why did I like the nickname he gave me so much?*

I didn't reply and continued to pry at his arm. He didn't care that a few eyes landed on our awkward situation or that I felt like an insect stuck in a spider's sticky web. But although the whole thing was awkward to an outsider, being in his grasp gave me comfort, and that was what hurt the most. My appetite had increased for how he treated me and knowing that I might mean nothing to him was like a punch to the gut. We finally moved on to another vendor, and his grip released.

"I'm going back to the suite," I said as I pressed the tablet into my chest.

He watched me walk around him, letting me get a

few feet before following in my direction. The bottom of his leather loafers sounded off the concrete floor, his pace picking up with each step. The elevators came into view, and I was sure he was going to stretch his hand and grab my arm, but he stopped when a low voice called his name. I continued to the elevators, refusing to turn around until I was standing in front of them. He stopped to talk to a man but made sure to slice his gaze over to me every few seconds.

They exchanged more words, including my name, and they both looked in my direction. They started over toward the elevators, and I turned my back and fidgeted with the tablet. Apparently, this guy's name was Dylan, he owned a tow company in Stonebridge, and he hadn't seen Aiden in years. Trying my best not to appear annoyed, I slammed my finger on the elevator button. The elevator doors chimed, and they said their goodbyes.

His hand found my waist, and he guided me into the elevator, slamming me against the wall. "Why is my baby girl so upset?" His warm breath tickled the peach fuzz on my cheek, sending a sheet of ice cracking down my spine.

I reverted my gaze to the floor and locked them on his shoes. He clipped a finger under my chin, and I sliced it away. My defying movements did nothing for him but turn him on. Low growls seeped off his tongue, and a knee-buckling smirk spread across his lips.

He caged his arms on both sides of my head and lowered his forehead to mine. I shouldn't want to kiss him, but I did, and I hate myself for it.

"If you don't tell me what's wrong, then I will have to use force."

His words made my eyes shoot up, and I found myself pushing at his chest as tears teased the corners of my eyes.

I released a shaky breath and dropped my hands to my side. "What?"

"I don't like secrets, so either you tell me, or I'll be forced to spank it out of you or worse." He lowered a thumb to my lips and separated them as he slid it inside. "Fuck it out of you."

My stomach went from slightly knotted to turning flips as we approached the suite door, but my back hit the wall before I could swipe my keycard, and his lips crashed onto mine.

CHAPTER 12
Truths & Trust ~ Aiden

I WAS ONLY worried about getting to the root of her dampened demeanor and comforting her. Every second that passed with my tongue down her throat sent my body into a charge. I pressed harder against her, pressing my raging cock into her stomach. She gasped once I broke our tether, and her eyes softened as she met my gaze. I grabbed her hand and slid the keycard over the reader. Once the door clicked, I pushed it open with my hip and dragged her inside. She resisted, and that was my cue to pin her against the wall with my pelvis. Her features changed like the seasons, once eyes so bright, now fogged with anger.

I couldn't help the smirk that spread across my face when she leaned into me, a sad attempt at trying to free herself from my hold. I took a step back, but my actions were swift, and before she had a chance to escape, I picked her up and forced my way between her legs. Her eyes widened, and she looked down, surprised that her legs were dangling in the air around my hips. The moment I saw her at the coffeehouse I knew I wanted her, but once she stepped foot in my office, there was no denying our attraction, even if our minds fought the desire early on. Ollie and I were two peas in a pod. She was made for me.

"Who…" Her words trailed off before she finished the sentence, and I pressed my forehead to hers.

I traced a thumb under her eye, stopping the fallen tear before it dripped down her cheek. "Whose who?"

She cut her glare past my shoulder, and I gave her ass a gentle squeeze to return her attention.

"Jenny." Her words came out shaky, and another roll of tears spilled over her lashes.

I blew out my cheeks and lifted my head to the ceiling in relief. Jogging my memory, I recalled the text message I got from my daughter earlier this morning, but I hadn't had time to reply.

I took her face in my palms and leaned into her. "Jenny is my 19-year-old daughter."

Her mouth fell open, and she drew her head back. "You have a daughter?" She pulled her bottom lip between her teeth before letting it slowly slip back out. "Do you have a wife too?" Her eyes narrowed.

I ran the bridge of my nose across her cheek and planted a kiss. "No, but I'll have one soon."

She didn't make light of my joke and rolled her big, beautiful chocolate eyes.

"Why didn't you tell me you had a daughter?"

"You never asked." I brushed a loose strand of hair from her face and traced my knuckle across her cheek. "I'm sorry, baby girl. I got a divorce six years ago. I was in a loveless marriage, but I stayed because of Jenny. I haven't been with anyone in over six years."

She bit the inside of her cheek, and I waited for her to collect her thoughts. She didn't need to tell me how she felt. I could see it clear as day in her eyes, and removing any doubts she harbored was my main priority.

"Oh, sorry, I freaked out. I just…"

I placed my finger on her lips and locked her gaze. "If someone had told me that the day Olivia Mason walked into my office was the day I would be given another opportunity to love, I would have laughed them off, but I'm in this for the long haul."

"But you just met me. How can I be all these things to you?"

"Because I've been in love before, and I know exactly what it feels like." I tucked my hands under her ass and walked toward the bedroom. "Now let daddy show you just how much he fucking loves you."

I dropped her down near the bed and let her watch me undress as I tore off every single piece of clothing like my life depended on it. I climbed onto the bed, leaned back into the soft pillows, and palmed my cock. Witnessing her hold on to her composure was the cutest thing.

I let out a low moan and thrust my hips. "Daddy's waiting."

She peeled at her clothes until she was down to her pink bra and panties. My cock ached for her. It ached to feel her warmth. Slipping off her undergarments, she stood nude on the side of the bed with her arms placed in front of her soft belly.

I crooked a finger in my direction. "Be a good girl."

The bed dipped as she placed one knee on the soft comforter, and then she stilled her movements. "Um, I'm…."

"I want you. All 220 pounds of you. Now sit on my fucking dick."

I took the liberty of memorizing her weight from her driver's license because I wanted to remind her on a daily basis that she was perfect in my eyes, no matter how much she weighs. Precum dripped down my shaft, and I palmed my throbbing cock one more time before she aligned her slit with the swollen bulb of my flesh.

"Sit." With my words clipped, I made sure she understood it was a demand and not a suggestion.

When the tip met her entrance, I growled and

grabbed ahold of her waist. She slid down like molasses, slow and steady. *Fuck me.*

She shifted a little and then stopped.

"Bad girl. Tsk Tsk," I chastised.

Her arms found her front, and she dipped her chin. "What?"

"I said sit. All the way down."

I knew she wasn't fully seated. My length stretched well beyond six inches, and I had a girth that would gobble her up whole. But nevertheless, she did as told and sat down.

"Hands behind your back," I said as I placed my arms above my head. "You'll never be able to hide from me, Ollie."

She pouted her cute little lips and placed her hands behind her back. I loved it when she did that. I let my lips peel into a wide grin as my eyes feasted upon her. I took my time as I let my cock warm in her tight cunt. Her cheeks turned a shade darker once she caught my gaze.

"Use your words, baby, talk to daddy."

She shifted. "How long do I have to sit here?"

"Until your ready to be daddy's little slut." I parted my lips just enough so she could see the glint of my tongue glide across my teeth.

She felt so damn good that I had to still my movement to prevent from filling her up.

"Do you think..." Her words trailed off, and she chewed on her bottom lip.

I lifted my hips and ran my hands up and down her soft thick thighs. "Yes?"

"Do you think your family will accept me? Us?" Her eyes sliced to my abs, and she traced a dainty finger over the grooves of my muscles.

I yanked her wrist, jolting her forward, and let my hand become tangled in her soft tresses. "I haven't given a fuck about what my family thinks of me in over twenty years, and I guarantee you I'm not about to start caring now.

"Oh. I just—"

"Shut up and ride my dick before I change my mind and bury my cock in your mouth instead."

She lifted slightly, and I chased after her hardened nipples, teasing them with my tongue. My actions forced soft moans off her lips, but I ached to hear her scream. She rocked slowly, nervousness settling in as she fought with her mind. I hated that she second guessed herself because she had no reason to. I placed my hands on her face, cupping her soft cheeks, and lifted my head until our foreheads touched.

"That's it. Take it all. Take every inch of me without remorse." I returned my hands to her nipples and pinched. Her moans were like music to my ears.

Her speed picked up, her breathing laboring as she settled into her stride. I didn't know what sound I liked more. The wetness of her cunt eating my flesh or the rugged moans dripping off her lips. Either way, it wasn't enough. I needed more. My name oozed off her tongue with hooded eyes, and my hand found her throat.

"Look at me while you fuck me," I demanded. I took over and wrapped her hair around my fist as my other hand found her throat. "Are you daddy's slut?"

Her pillow-soft breasts teased me as her body jolted from each thrust, and I engraved the image into my brain. I didn't let up and pulled her down until her hair became a veil around us. Then, with our eyes locked, my hands found the luscious mounds of her ass cheeks and gripped. The sound of her unexpected gasp when I emptied her out nearly sent me over the edge, but once the word "daddy" slipped off her lips as I slammed back in sent me into ruins. I held her down like a vice as I fed her everything I had, and the thought of ever letting her go scared the shit out of me.

"You're such a good girl. You made daddy come so hard." I placed a kiss on her forehead and gently placed her next to me.

She waited with tired limbs and wild hair as I gathered a warm towel and a glass of cool water. Spreading her legs with my hand, I cleaned her up, and a soft giggle escaped her lips.

"Does it tickle?" I said as I lowered my head

between her legs and teased my tongue down the center of her folds.

She bit down on her bottom lip and tried to shove my head away, but her resistance was only making me hungrier.

"I'm sore," She whimpered.

I lifted and closed her legs before placing the cover over her. "You won't be tomorrow, though." I winked and placed another kiss on her cheek.

CHAPTER 13
New Beginnings ~ Olivia

I WOKE to Aiden already out of bed and fully dressed. The man reminded me of a walking espresso machine. He kept me awake all night, forcing me to ride him over and over again. He had the stamina of a horse with a large appetite. He ate every inch of my body, and I let him. Every time I dozed off, I would wake to his tongue wedged between my folds, greedily consuming me.

Being in his arms was surreal and nothing like I had ever experienced. A part of me didn't want to believe it. How could one man, a man that I met a few days ago, make me feel like this, like the most amazing person in the world. His heavy footsteps slid across the carpet, and the bed dipped when he sat beside me. His exclusive scent seeped into my nostrils.

"I have to go talk to a few more vendors. It shouldn't take too long." He brushed my wild hair out of my face and trailed a thumb down my cheek.

I shifted and pulled the covers up until only my eyes were exposed. The fabric of his shirt strained against his muscles with each movement, and I locked my eyes on his brawny biceps.

"Are you sore?" he whispered before easing in to place a kiss between my brows.

I lowered the cover. "No." *I lied.*

He'd battered my insides, leaving my folds tender, my nipples sore, and my legs heavier than bricks.

Light strains of his deep laughter peppered the air. "Well, that just means tomorrow I'll have to fuck you harder." He stood and walked over to the desk. "We have a couple of hours before we leave." He waved the brochure for the spa in his hand, and I sprang up.

"What time do we leave?"

"We need to be on the jet by 6:45 p.m."

Another soft kiss found the top of my head, and he turned to head out the door. I checked the clock next to the bed and threw back the covers. I had never been to a spa before, and this one was state of the art with all the bells and whistles. I took a shower and packed my suitcase, setting it next to Aidens near the door. Slipping into a soft t-shirt and jeans, I gobbled down the yummy brunch and headed to the spa.

THE THUMP of the jet landing on the tarmac woke me from my sleep, and Aiden slid his hand and up down my back as I lifted my head. Cradled in his arms, he found my gaze and kissed my lips softly. A heaviness settled in my chest as reality slapped me in the face.

The resort was a nice escape from my everyday life, but now that was all over. I placed my hand on Aiden's chest, and he brought my fingers to his lips. I liked what we had, our chemistry, the way he made me feel, but I worried about the string that tethered us together, wondering if it would break. Not only was Aiden old enough to be my dad, but we were from two different worlds. He had it all, and I literally had nothing.

As gloomy thoughts swam through my head, I cut my gaze to the window in an attempt to hide the worry on my face. The jet came to a complete stop, and the lights flickered on. I squinted and climbed off Aiden's lap. Slugging down the steps, I waited by the car as the driver loaded the luggage into the trunk. The beat of my pulse increased by the minute as thoughts of Damien crept back into my mind. The ride back to Stonebridge from the airport didn't take long. Aiden used the time to catch up on the emails I couldn't answer, and I kept my gaze to the window, taking in the blackened sky. When the car slowed to exit the freeway, I shot Aiden a strange look.

"Yes, baby girl?" he asked as he rested his hand on my thigh.

"Is the driver lost?" I asked as I took another glance out the window.

He gave a sheepish grin and slid his fingers into my hair. "Not at all. He's headed home."

I traded a glance between the driver and Aiden and tilted my head. "Whose home?"

"Ours."

My mouth fell open at his words, leaving a string of jumbled syllables falling off my tongue. I didn't know how to respond to his comment. My mind turned to mush. The car pulled up to the garage gates, and blackness cloaked us as we descended. Rows of luxury vehicles lined the garage walls before stopping in front of two golden french doors. Gearing up to force a sentence past my lips, Aiden pushed open the car door and grabbed me by the arm. I followed behind him blindly through the golden doors and into a lobby that looked like the inside of a palace. Aiden's lips fell into a cunning smirk, and he kept his eyes on me as the elevator whisked us to the top floor. Intertwining his fingers with mine, he guided me toward the lonely door at the end of the hall.

"Aiden, I can't—"

"Shut up," he interrupted, then separated my lips with his tongue for a quick mouthwatering kiss.

Looking down at his phone, he unlocked it with his thumb and shuffled through the apps until he landed on an icon in the shape of a house. Although a small cloud of uncertainty loomed over me, elation slowly rippled to the surface. The door clicked, and he pushed the door open and stepped aside. Extending his arm for me to do the honors, I released a breath and entered. Stepping out of my flats, the heat from the wood warmed my soles. His house reminded me of a modern-day oasis wrapped in a sheet of coziness and warmth.

My eyes landed on the floor-to-ceiling windows that overlooked Stonebridge. Hints of cinnamon and wood impaled my lungs with each breath, and I let my fingers graze across the leather furniture. I walked in circles, taking in everything before sinking into the oversized leather couch. I let my head fall back and met Aidens stare. It felt like home.

"It's big enough for Oreo," I said as I trailed my gaze around the living room once more.

"So? Will you stay?" He sauntered over and scratched the edge of his grin as he lowered himself between my legs.

I pierced my lips and raised my shoulders. "Mmm. I suppose."

Relief suffused his features, and he clipped a finger under my chin. "Good girl."

CHAPTER 14
Love & Forced to C*m ~ Olivia

THREE MONTHS LATER...

I SHIFTED and leaned back on my heels. Legs spread, hands bound, and mouth gagged. That's how he liked it when we worked from home every Thursday. The night he asked me to move in with him, I said yes, and he immediately had everything from my shitty apartment moved into his condo. It was probably the fastest move in history.

In less than two hours, the movers piled everything I owned in the foyer. He promised that I wouldn't have to step foot in that neighborhood ever again and ensured that my ex would no longer be a problem I had to fear. Oreo loved her new home, along with the luxury pampering Aiden provided her.

Not only did she get Fur Baby Delight treats every day, she became a regular at the pet spa.

His overly protective nature resulted in him installing a state of the art alarm system in the condo and hiring extra security just for me. I told him he didn't have to do all of that, but he insisted.

His deep laughter made my pulse quicken, even though his attention wasn't directed at me. I melted under him, succumbing to his dangerous and deliciously sinful ways. His control over me was rooted in protection and love, which I'd craved for so long. I shifted again, adjusting my spine as I dug my knees into the soft plush carpet below me. He had a habit of keeping me on my knees, and I enjoyed stretching my neck to meet his gaze.

He swiveled around in his chair and stilled his movements. His gaze unyielding on the steady stream of saliva running down my chin. When he first gaged me, I had been adamant about swallowing the pool of saliva that settled in my mouth to lessen the embarrassment, but watching me drool was something he loved. His flesh awoke to the sight of my vulnerability, the way heat crept in my cheeks as he made me his little slut. He pulled the earpiece out and placed the conference call on speaker, making sure to hit the mute button before returning his attention back to me.

He preferred to work from home on Thursdays due to all the online meetings, and he liked to give his staff an early start on the weekend. Most of the high-profile clients he protected ended their workweek on Thursday and jetted off to other destinations for the weekend. He rested an elbow on the arm of the chair, locking our gaze as he rested a finger over his lips. The anticipation killed me, just like it did every time I was in this position. His actions were wicked and merciless. He gave me everything I needed, including leaving my pussy soaking wet and lips swollen as I pleaded for more.

"Aren't you being patient?" The corner of his lips lifted, and he leaned in.

I lifted my chin, widened my eyes, and straightened my spine. The steady stream of drool made its way down the cleavage of my breasts and onto my stomach. He watched with steady eyes as he salivated at the mouth. He leaned in closer, assuring I got a whiff of my favorite cologne, and then teased my nipples with his fingers. They pebbled, then he pinched. A light cry pushed past the gag, causing more drool to seep out the corners.

He dropped his hands and returned them back to his lap. "Have you been a good girl, Ollie? Are you getting good grades?"

Eager to get his hands back on my sensitive nipples, I nodded, then jutted my chest out. Once he made me his, he made sure I was his equal. He removed me from the administrative role and added me as co-owner to his firm, securing me with a healthy financial future. He enrolled me into the best online college of security and IT because he wanted more than a pretty face; he wanted a partner. Jasper didn't mind; he was actually relieved because now he had an excuse to pursue his own career goals. He wasn't a fan of the private security sector but had gone along with it for Aiden's sake.

He turned, reaching over to grab his tablet off the desk. "You are so fucking, smart, baby. Daddy is so proud of you." He returned his stare to the tablet that revealed my grades and gently placed it back on the desk. "Do you want daddy to make you feel good?"

I nodded with force, and he reached over to the last drawer on the left side of his desk. Heat flared through me, drenching my panties in wetness. Impressing daddy yielded great rewards, and I was eager to receive my benefits. He pulled my favorite vibrator from the depths of his drawer and teetered it in front of my face. I widened my legs and forced my ass to the ground. My thighs stung. Being a bigger girl had challenges, but I didn't mind taking them.

"When I'm done with you, I'm going to fuck your brains out on this desk." He hovered the head of the vibrator below my bottom lip, catching the stream of drool.

He made sure it was fully coated and then pulled it away. The buzz reminded me of a million bees, and my heart drummed rapidly in my chest as his fingers pulled the crotch of my panties to the side. The intense vibration made me gasp, and just like the teaser he was, he pulled it away. Every nerve in my body stood on pins and needles as he played puppeteer with my orgasm.

"Fuck, moan for daddy. Let me hear how fucking good it feels." The familiar smooth tone of his voice evaporated into thin air, leaving behind something gritty and salacious.

He worked me, making sure to wear me down as he brought me to my high, only to steal it away repeatedly. The first time I experienced edge play, I cried out of frustration, but he made me love it and crave it. He made me beg and listened to my pleas as if they were music to his ears. The feeling was mutual, my cries turned him on, and his moans turned me on. He palmed my breasts, teasing my nipples between his finger and thumb. Pinching and tugging as he held a steady hand to my cunt. I knew what he was waiting for, and when tears pricked the corners of my eyes, a smirk touched his lips.

"That's it. That's what daddy wants to see. Tears of pleasure. Fuck baby. You're so damn sexy."

He pulled away, and my chest heaved. My pussy wept, and my thighs burned, but I wanted more. More pleasure, more daddy. I whined to get his attention, and he brought the tip of the vibrator to his lips and waited until a drop of his saliva met the smooth silicone.

He returned it back to its rightful place between my folds and pressed it against my sensitive clit. "Too bad your gagged, baby girl. I would love to watch you taste your juices." He pressed his nose to the side of my cheek and let a low moan seep into my ear. "Are you ready to come for daddy, baby girl?"

He fisted my hair, and with a gentle tug, my neck extended. Lust blindsided me, and my body convulsed at his words. His fingers found the latch on the gag, and he unclipped it, allowing my compressed moan to penetrate the air. Meeting me at eye level, he fell to his knees and pulled me into his chest. Out of breath with sore folds, he held me tight as he massaged my scalp. I waited for my high to cease before pulling away. A stain soaked his shirt, and I placed my palm over it.

"Oops," I said as I fidgeted with the wet spot.

He took my face in his palms and lifted. "Fuck, I'm so happy you're mine."

A Sneak Peek at: Daddy's Breeder

IT WAS 4am when my phone rang. It wasn't a text. Someone was actually calling me at four in the morning. I blindly reached over to my nightstand, fumbling for it before it vibrated off the table.

Lincoln. Of course.

At 25, my brother was four years older than me but still lived the all-gas-no-breaks lifestyle of a high schooler. Welcome to the world of the younger, more responsible sibling.

"What did you do this time?" I mumbled.

"Brook. I'm in jail."

Of course, you are.

"Are you for real right now?!" I whine. "I do not have the money to bail your ass out, Link. Wait it out."

Edging to toss my phone back on the nightstand, his next sentence made me freeze.

"They think I robbed a gas station, Brook. With a gun."

I sprung up from the bed, his words waking me up like a defibrillator. "Wait, what?"

"I'm being accused of armed robbery," he choked out.

"Did you do it?" I asked.

"I don't own a gun," he snapped back.

I squeezed my eyes shut and tried to sort it all out in my head. Lincoln had been in trouble a lot over the years. The foster care system wasn't kind to either of us and once he hit high school, he rebelled in every way he could. Since dropping out of high school and emancipating himself at sixteen, he's been in and out of jail a handful of times, though usually for petty things like possession of marijuana or peeing on cop cars. But this was serious.

"Okay, just sit tight," I tell him as I flipped my comforter from my legs.

"What the fuck else am I going to do?" His words were dripped in sarcasm. *He's scared.* Snarkiness was his defense mechanism.

"Lincoln, just hold on, okay?" I say calmly as I get up and grab a pair of ripped jeans and a baby Yoda t-shirt. "I'm going to come down there, and we will sort it all out."

Daddy's Breeder

CHAPTER 1
Old Habits Die Hard - Brooklyn

IT WAS 4 a.m. when my phone rang. It wasn't a text. Someone was actually calling me at four in the morning. I blindly reached over to my nightstand, fumbling for it before it vibrated off the table.

Lincoln. Of course.

At 25, my brother was four years older than me but still lived the all-gas-no-brakes lifestyle of a high schooler. Welcome to the world of the younger, more responsible sibling.

"What did you do this time?" I mumbled.

"Brook. I'm in jail."

Of course, you are.

"Are you for real right now?!" I whine. "I do not have the money to bail your ass out, Link. Wait it out."

Edging to toss my phone back on the nightstand, his next sentence made me freeze.

"They think I robbed a gas station, Brook. With a gun."

I sprung up from the bed, his words waking me up like a defibrillator. "Wait, what?"

"I'm being accused of armed robbery," he choked out.

"Did you do it?" I asked.

"I don't own a gun," he snapped back.

I squeezed my eyes shut and tried to sort it all out in my head. Lincoln had been in trouble a lot over the years. The foster care system wasn't kind to either of us, and once he hit high school, he rebelled in every way he could. Since dropping out and emancipating himself at sixteen, he's been in and out of jail a handful of times, though usually for petty things like possession of marijuana or peeing on cop cars. But this was serious.

"Okay, just sit tight," I told him as I flipped my comforter from my legs.

"What the fuck else am I going to do?" His words dripped in sarcasm. *He's scared.* Snarkiness was his defense mechanism.

"Lincoln, just hold on, okay?" I say calmly as I get up and grab a pair of ripped jeans and a baby Yoda t-shirt. "I'm going to come down there, and we will sort it all out."

TWO WEEKS HAD PASSED since Lincoln's arrest, and of course, I didn't get it *sorted out*. We couldn't afford the bail, and Lincoln's shitty lawyer wasn't any help except for warning us about shady bail bond schemes. So Lincoln sat in jail while I worked to find a competent lawyer. Turns out, lawyers, good ones, cost almost as much as the bail itself. Dead ended, I'd settled on putting my trust in the shitty public defender for the time being. But I visited Lincoln as often as I could. Unfortunately, between my waitress job at Estelle's Cafe and attending college full time, I missed a lot of visitation hours.

Today though, Lincoln had called me, desperate for me to come in. I succumbed to his request and took off from work early, something I knew I'll pay for in lack of grocery money next week. After packing a few of Lincoln's favorite snacks, I headed out the door to my '91 Jeep Wrangler.

The engine belted out its usual labored cough before turning over, and I flipped the lights on, making my way down the street. The Jeep had been a gift from the last foster home I'd stayed at. The Jeep was old, painted a flat lemon yellow. There were rust spots around the edges, and none of the hubcaps matched. As I made my way down the street with Doja Cat blasting from the speakers, my eyes began to burn with tears as memories made their way to the surface. In my twenty-one years of life, I have lived through the struggles of what felt like five lives. But there were two constants: My Jeep. And Lincoln. And I couldn't afford to lose either.

I pulled up to the jail and parked in the visitor lot. After signing my name on the dotted line and going through security, I followed the rest of the human cattle into the common area where we all waited. A loud buzzer sounded, making my shoulders jump, and I stood once I caught sight of Lincoln. He found a table near the back, and I walked over.

"I don't care what people say. Orange is not the new black. You look like shit, bro." I set down his bag of goodies and settled onto the hard bench.

"Yeah, well, I'm in jail for a crime I didn't commit," he said, taking a drag of his cigarette as he pried open the small bag of hot Cheetos. He tilted his head and exhaled. "Any luck finding me a new lawyer?"

"Oh, yeah, sure. Let me just add up the tips I got last night serving chicken fried steak to a group of seedy truckers, and I'll get right on that."

Lincoln narrowed his eyes as he held my gaze and smashed his cigarette into the small ashtray. "The d-bag representing me is doing a shit job, Brook. I don't even think he believes my story. I need a reputable lawyer, or I'm fucked."

I swallowed and let my shoulders slump forward. The attitude I was throwing at him was all smoke and mirrors. Honestly, it terrified me whenever I thought about Lincoln's situation. Although we bickered and complained like mortal enemies, I couldn't deny that he was the reason I survived foster care and all the other shit that came my way. He was why I had the drive to graduate high school with a 3.8 GPA. The reason I believed in myself was enough to push my way into college. *I needed him.*

He must have seen the emotion surfacing in my eyes because his expression softened. He reached across the table, taking my hand in both of his. "Listen, sis, I know it seems impossible. But I also know you. You always find a way. And right now, I really, *really* need a way out."

I nodded, blinking back the tears threatening to spill over my lashes. The buzzer sounded again, a harsh reminder that visitation was short-lived. I stood and let go of Lincoln's hand. A slither of hope rested in his eyes, and it hurt like hell to see it because I had no idea how I was going to get him out of jail.

I walked back to my Jeep and made my way home. Stonebridge was a small city nestled about three hours outside of Chicago. It was the best of both worlds with a bustling downtown and quaint main street vibes.

But like everywhere else, it had its nice parts and its less than desirable parts.

My apartment fell into the latter category. I parked behind a building with eroding brick walls and barred windows. Climbing out of the Jeep, I slammed the door shut as I ignored the sirens in the distance. Hoping to make it to my front door without a hiccup, I heard a whistle, and against my better judgment, I looked back over my shoulder and eyed a couple of men leaning against the side of the building.

"Hey there, kitty cat," one of them called.

"How much for a ride, baby?" the other one chimed in.

I ignored their advances and hurried inside. Powering up the two flights of rickety stairs, I pulled open the door and sauntered down the hallway to my apartment. Fumbling with the keys, they dropped out of my hands, and I squeezed my eyes shut as tears forced their way through the corners. The weight on my shoulders was enough to crush me. Yet even if it did, I still wouldn't get a break.

I made my way to the kitchen, popping a cup of ramen in the microwave before grabbing the one wine glass I owned and filled it with wine from the box on the counter. My entire life was ironic, really. My wine costs more than my dinner. *Priorities.*

Playing catchup with the cast of *Bridgerton*, I twirled my fork into my noodles and shoved them into my mouth. Ready to repeat my actions once more, the chime of my phone stole my attention, and my screen lit up. A notification from the latest dating app my best friend Mallory signed me up for slid across my screen, and I rolled my eyes, but still, I couldn't look away. I begrudgingly swiped my thumb across the screen, and my eyes locked on a man who looked to be in his thirties with dark hair and brown eyes. I mean, he wasn't not attractive...

I clicked on the message he sent. "Nice headshot. Love the red hair. Does the carpet match the drapes?"

Shaking my head, I tossed my phone aside and sank into the torn cushions of the couch.

CHAPTER 2
Perfect Stranger - Brooklyn

"WE SHOULD GO OUT FRIDAY NIGHT," my best friend Mallory said from the passenger seat of my Jeep. I gave her rides to work because she and her boyfriend shared a car, and their work schedules clashed. In return, she paid for the gas. It was a nice tradeoff, honestly.

"Hello?" she said as she shut the overhead mirror and flipped up the visor, smacking her freshly glossed lips together. "Did you hear what I said? I want to go out on Friday. I need to get drunk."

"Sorry," I said, coming to the stoplight. "We can do that."

I pulled my phone out and scrolled through until I found my banking app, but before I could open it, she waved her hand across the screen.

"Don't worry about it. Just dress hot, and I'm sure

we won't pay for any of our own alcohol." She grinned and pulled her bottom lip between her teeth.

I found it odd that she went out so much and flirted her way from free cocktail to free cocktail. It was one thing to do that when you're single. But she and her boyfriend had been exclusive for eight months. Waiting for the longest light to flip to green, I killed the last few seconds and pressed on my baking app. My stomach turned over as I focused on the big negative $40 in bright red. *Damn internet bill.* The light turned green, and I tossed my phone aside and blinked back tears that teased the corners of my eyes.

"Imagine a world where money didn't matter." She reached over and pinched my love handles in an attempt to make me laugh.

I forced my lips into a smile and pushed the worry that wanted to wash over me to the back of my brain.

"You know my ex-roommate's sister-in-law has this cousin who made enough money in one weekend to pay 3 months' worth of bills?"

I narrowed my eyes and passed a few quick glances her way. "Doing what?"

She shrugged as she picked at her cuticles. "She's an escort."

Her words came out so casually that I almost choked on the spit pooling in my mouth. I returned my gaze to the road ahead and slowed as we turned the corner. "You're not serious?" I said as I darted my eyes between her and the road.

"I am. She works for some madam. It's almost like a dating app, honestly. Except you get paid to get laid." She laughed as the words spilled off her tongue.

I'm not laughing. "Is that even legal?"

"People do it." She shrugged and popped her freshly glossed lips together as we pulled into the cafe's parking lot.

"They're...hookers," I said with more disgust than intended. The idea of it made my stomach sour. I mean, I wasn't a virgin, but the idea of doing it for money with any ole man who paid the fee was disgusting, degrading, and just weird.

"They prefer to be called escorts." Her tone seemed sharper, and she winged a brow. "I don't know. I'd probably do it if I wasn't hopelessly devoted to my boyfriend."

My mouth dropped open. "You're not serious, Mal."

"Why not?" The passenger door whined as she swung it open and dropped her leg out. "It's easy money. Might as well get paid $1000 for doing something you would do for free with some lame guy from the bar."

So much of her sentence shocked me, but the last part had me second-guessing my thoughts. "$1000 a night...?"

Her lips curled into a salacious grin, and she nodded. "And that's not even in the big leagues. Some men will pay up to four grand an evening if they like you." She unclasped her seatbelt and turned to face me. "Just hear me out. Hypothetically. You get a job as an *escort*," the word dripped from her mouth like honey as she attempted to glam it up, "you do it for a couple nights. A couple weeks tops. And you're debt-free. Worry-free. Stress-free."

I couldn't even begin to wrap my brain around the whole idea. In two nights, the money I'd make would be more than the money I made in two whole months from the cafe. All my problems could be fixed.

"Still. It's paid sex." I shook my head and turned off the Jeep.

Mallory shrugged. "Think about it. It's a lot of money for very little effort."

I wanted to say there's nothing to think about. The idea was insane. Negative forty dollars or not. We made our way inside, and I hung my purse on the hook in the back room. Then I took a deep breath and headed into Estelle's office. Estelle and her friend Iris owned this cafe and a handful of coffee shops in Stonebridge. They were a best friend duo and served the best coffee and grilled cheeses I had ever tasted.

"Hey?" I knocked on the open door as I leaned a hip into the door frame.

She looked up from her desk. "Brooklyn! Just the

girl I wanted to see. You still up for working doubles this weekend?" She perched her cat-like ruby red colored frames up her nose and waited for my reply.

I nodded. "Sure." I let a beat of awkward silence pass as my stomach twisted in knots. "So... I was just wondering about that raise I asked about."

She set her pen down, and her features soften. I knew that look, and it gutted me.

"Listen, hun. I know I said you guys would be getting better pay soon. Especially you. You're my hardest working waitress. But we have to update our refrigerators to meet the state's standards. And with the espresso machine being on the fritz at one of our coffee shops, I'm going to have to hold off on those raises for a bit longer."

I chewed the inside of my cheek as I swallowed her words. Trying to fight back the tears, I fidgeted with the apron and then folded my arms across my chest.

She tilted her head and raised her brows. "Just for a couple months. Promise."

I walked out to find Mallory trying to manage the small afternoon rush that came hurdling in. With my brain in a fog, my body went into robot mode as I helped with the rush. Eviction was very real right now. But I couldn't even worry about my home when my mind was stuck on Lincoln's situation. He didn't have a couple of months. His trial was fast approaching, and he still didn't have a lawyer. The thought of him spending fifteen years in jail for a crime he didn't even commit turned my blood to sludge. My stomach twisted and turned, and my feet were hightailing it toward the restroom in a blink of an eye. Twisting my hips through the sea of tables, a hand reached out and tugged my arm.

"I'm ready to order. The other waitress said this is your section."

My section? This is not my section. I shot Mallory a look, and she bit her lip before letting a smirk crawl across her lips.

Annoyed, I made eye contact with him for the first time. "Yeah, sorry, what would you li..." I trailed off.

He was a beast of a man, probably 6'3 at the least, with solid lean muscle. A dress shirt buttoned to the very top struggled to conceal his muscles. He flexed an arm as he lifted the menu, and I was certain they were bigger than one of my thighs. He had dark brown hair, short on the sides, and moussed messily on top with a scruffy jawline that could cut glass. Although every inch of this man froze me in my tracks, it was his eyes that melted my spine. The color fell between hazel and grey, dark-rimmed on the outside and stormy on the inside.

He raised a thick, dramatic eyebrow. "Hello?"

"Yes, sorry, what?" I asked as I cleared my throat.

A small smirk tempted the corners of his mouth. "I asked, what's good here?"

"Oh, right." I fumbled with my folder, pulling out the list of our daily specials on a crisp white and gold card.

Estelle's cafe caught the eye of many business professionals due to its contemporary airy feel and light lunch menu. Of course, I dropped it on the floor. I bent to pick it up, and I swear I saw his eyes follow my butt in the movement. His eyes locked onto mine when I stood up, and he traced a finger over his mouth. Heat crept into my cheeks, and words fumbled off my lips.

"We have a wedge salad topped with bacon, blue cheese crumbles, grape tomatoes, and a balsamic drizzle. It's served with grilled sirloin. We also have The Bomb-Ass Chicken, which—"

"I'm sorry, the what?" he asked.

"The Bomb-Ass Chicken. Our cook named it. It's grilled chicken with honey mustard, bacon, sautéed mushrooms, and sharp cheddar cheese," I said.

The look on his face let me know he wasn't convinced, and he sliced his gaze back to the menu in search of something else more edible and with a normal name.

"Which do you prefer?" he asked, his voice low and gritty.

"I like it all," I blurted out. I regretted the words immediately when his subtle smirk tugged into a lopsided grin as his eyes raked over me. As if to say, *of course, you do.*

"I'll go with the club sandwich." He flipped the menu card back over before sliding it in my direction.

"Any sides with that?" I kept my eyes on the pad, refusing to get lost in his intoxicating gaze.

"Like?" His words dangled in the air.

Trying to sound like an intelligent human being and not one who hadn't learned to speak, I inhaled before rambling off the most basic options. "Umm, fries or fruit or something sweeter..."

"Sweeter?" The gritty yet dignified flow of his words made me catch his gaze.

I blushed involuntarily and pathetically.

I took his order back to the kitchen before he even responded to my question about sides and stuck the sheet onto the hook. *What the hell was that?* Men usually never threw me off, but something about this one had my palms sweaty and pulse racing. I took a deep breath to calm my nerves when the door flew open.

"Holy hell, talk about a snack!" Mallory blurted out before the kitchen door even swung shut.

I gave her a look, my face heating up all over again. I patted my apron down, straightened my ponytail, and pretended I was capable of acting normal. "If you're so into him, why did you give the table to me? He's in your section."

"Because I have a boyfriend." She rolled her eyes. "Besides, I felt like you needed something exciting in your day considering the shitshow that is your life." Her words came out casually and truthfully as she applied a thin coat of gloss to her lips.

"Wow, thanks, Mal," I grumbled.

"Lighten up. Have fun with it."

Fun. Right. What even was that? I buzzed from table to table, all while the man with the dreamy eyes chatted with another guy while he picked at his club sandwich. Even though preoccupied with a conversation, his eyes still found mine occasionally, and it sent shivers down my spine. Becoming more self-aware of the state of my attire, which included a soft cream-colored polo paired with slightly ripped dark denim blue jeans that exposed my elephant ankles. I found myself looking down at my appearance, and when I looked back up, his eyes locked on mine. I continued to hop from table to table, wondering every three seconds if he was still staring at me. I casually dropped the check on the man's table before heading to the kitchen to grab the next order. Busy with another rush, it wasn't until I stopped to catch my breath that I noticed he had left, and I swiped up the receipt and tip. My breath hitched in my throat as I stared down at the two crisp one hundred dollar bills. Did he do this on purpose? His tab was only $18.67 But then I saw the note on the receipt.

Next time I'll come back for something sweeter.

I realized my mouth was on the ground and snapped it shut.

"Is there something wrong?" Mal asked as she rounded the long counter.

I shook my head and shoved the money into the pocket of my apron. We were supposed to split tips. It was an odd rule considering most restaurants let individual servers keep the cash from their own tables. But Estelle liked to be inclusive, whatever that meant.

"Did he not tip?" Mallory placed her hands on her hips and folded her arms across her chest in protest.

"No, he didn't." Ignoring the devil that perched his ass on my shoulder, I shrugged and walked through the swinging door to the kitchen.

I LISTENED to Mallory talk about all the assholes she dealt with on the ride home. She complained about it after every shift, yet she never looked for another job.

I pulled up to her house, and before I could put the Jeep in park, her seatbelt flew back, and she twisted in my direction.

"You doing okay?"

No. I'm not. Even though the money in my pocket will, without a doubt, help me sleep a tiny bit better tonight, it's not even the tip of the iceberg. My eyes tear up as a response.

"Oh honey." She put her hand on my knee. "It's going to get better. Life always gets better."

"Does it, though?" I choked out. "Mine seems to get worse. It's always been this way. One step forward, four leaps back. I can't catch a break and now with Lincoln's lawyer issue..." I let my words trail off and buried my face in my hand.

"Here." She tapped my shoulder before returning her hands to her pink wallet.

"Oh, no, I don't want—"

"I *insist*." She stuffed the twenty-dollar bill in my hand. "Get some ice cream. Wine. Hell, go buy some weed if you want. Just take care of yourself, okay?"

I don't know where it came from or what possessed me to say it, but as she started to get out of the Jeep, I grabbed her arm.

My mouth opened, closed, and opened again. "What's the name of that agency? The...escort one?" I whispered the last part as if someone could hear me.

Mallory burst out in laughter, which soon subsided once she saw the seriousness etched into my features. She raised a brow, and I cut my gaze back to the street. We sat in silence as we processed the utterly ridiculous idea. An idea I hated to my core, but it seemed like the only way to help my brother.

"Really?" she asked, leaning into me.

I didn't say anything and eventually lowered my eyes to my lap. A hefty sigh made her shoulders rise. "Okay, I'll get the info and text you in a few."

I drove home with my heart pounding in my chest. I didn't regret asking for the information, and a small part of me became anxious, curious about what the process was like. I parked my car, and double checked the locks before getting out and heading toward my apartment. My phone vibrated as I approached my door, and my heart sank into my stomach. The knob was loose, meaning someone tried to break in. *Great.* I pushed my way in. Everything looked more or less normal. Probably because I had nothing to steal unless my collection of a boyband and baby Yoda t-shirts appealed to someone.

Certain that no one was hiding in a closet, I double-checked the locks and kicked my shoes off before crashing down into the couch. I opened the text and found the number for the agency staring back at me.

I needed better and so did Lincoln. I didn't have a choice.

CHAPTER 3
Point of no Return ~ Brooklyn

I SPENT most of the night tossing and turning, slipping in and out of restless sleep. Buried dreams of Lincoln's fate and being evicted plucked away at me, but the dream that ripped me from my sleep was the guy from the cafe. His sinister smirk and dreamy eyes found their way into my brain and left my panties in a small pool of wetness. The fact that I was even thinking about him made me smother a pillow over my face. Not only was I thinking about spreading my legs for a few thousand dollars, but I also added salt to the wound by lusting over a man old enough to be my father. He had to be in his early forties. But that smirk that tugged at the corners of his mouth as his eyes raked over me had me fantasizing about what it would feel like if his hands were raking over me, and in my dream, he was doing just that. I'd only been with a couple of guys, but every experience was one disappointment after another. However, this dream ended in me having to change my sheets.

I glanced at my phone. I didn't work today, but I got up anyway, afraid of what might happen if I went back to sleep. I made a cup of instant coffee and sat down on the couch. I pulled out my phone and eyed the number Mallory sent to me last night. Holding in a breath, I dialed the number and hit send before I could chicken out. The phone rang, and as each second passed, I secretly hoped it wasn't a real number or that it was disconnected. God, what if some gritty man answered? I didn't think men ran these kinds of things. Hell, I didn't know. I've never even thought about escort services outside of movies or in places like Las Vegas.

"Thank you for calling *Crème de la Crème*." A sultry woman's voice came over the line. "What is your 4-digit access code, please?"

My stomach bottomed out, and I pressed the end call button. Awesome. This was going great. I mentally kicked myself and called back again. I could do this. I could be a ho--- *Escort*.

The same woman answered, and I cleared my throat. The words tumbled out of my mouth. "My friend gave me this number. I need to speak with the Madam."

"Hold, please," she said, and soft elevator music poured through the line.

Well, at least it was classier than I had expected. It didn't help that I was nervous and sweating bullets. I squirmed around a bit, fidgeting with my hair, and twirled a lock around my finger.

"Miss?" the same voice asked. "The Madam has an interview opening at 8:50 this morning."

I glanced at the time on my phone and confirmed that I only had two hours to get ready. "Okay," I stuttered.

"The address is 7769 Hart Avenue," she rattled off.

I scrambled for a pen, not wanting to ask her again. I found a red Sharpie in the depth of my couch cushions but no paper, so I scribbled it down on my thigh in a frenzy.

"Please bring your ID. You are over 18, right?" she asks.

"Yes," I said.

"And what color is your hair?" she asked.

"Auburn…" I said, unsure why that even mattered.

"So redhead. Got it."

I opened my mouth to say something, but the line went dead before I could push the words out. I set my phone down on the small coffee table in front of me and listened as my heart pounded in my chest. The beating was literally turning my body numb. This was it. I couldn't back out if I wanted. A lump rose in my throat, my pulse slammed against my neck, all the signs of a breakdown coming full charge, but then it occurred to me that I didn't have time to fall to pieces.

    I got up and hurried over to my closet and flipped the light on. I hadn't even gotten the job yet but felt like I had lost it as I scanned my very lean closet from left to right. I didn't own much because every penny I got went to survival needs. I let my fingers float over the worn fabrics of my t-shirts, ripped jeans, and over-washed yoga pants. My only saving grace was the little black dress I wore to job interviews and funerals. It was the kind of thing you wore when you wanted people to take you seriously, not when you wanted to look sexy. Still, it was all I had. I tugged on it before seeing the shimmer of purple behind it. Hanging behind my funeral dress was a midnight colored cocktail dress that I borrowed from Mallory last year when we went to a dinner that her boyfriend had paid for. I had forgotten to give it back. I showered, ran a brush through my wild, thick curls, and closed my eyes as I stepped into the dress. Sucking in my belly for dear life, I opened my eyes in shock when I was able to bend over without fear that the seams would rip apart across my ass. I took a quick glance at my body in the mirror and, for some reason, found it hard to look myself in the face. Probably because of what I was about to do.

"It's for Lincoln," I reminded myself and grabbed my keys off the kitchen counter.

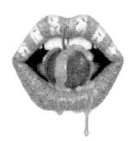

THE ADDRESS LED me to a posh little tea house in the nicer part of Stonebridge. The ritzy end. Honestly, I didn't get up here much. For one, I had no reason to. I couldn't afford half these uppity shops and cute cafes, so why torture myself? I parked my Jeep and made my way inside. I didn't see anyone sitting by themselves, so I assumed I got there first. My eyes scanned over the menu and then the price. They had everything from hot teas, by the cup or pot, to an array of fancy baked goods that cost more than my weekly coffee bill. My mouth watered as I looked at the colorful menu. Giving up a week's worth of grocery money for a few of these desserts was becoming more tempting by the second.

"See anything that catches your eye?" A frail girl with chestnut hair in a floral dress and frilly apron asked from behind the counter.

"Everything," I said with a small smile that faded as I pointed to the beverage fountain behind her. "Can I just have water for now? I'm meeting someone."

"Of course." A sugary smile settled on her face as she grabbed a clear cup from the tower next to her.

I glanced around, taking in the room. It reminded me of Estelle's cafe, just more expensive.

"Cucumber or lemon?" the girl asked.

I spun back around. "I'm sorry?"

"In your water. We have cucumber and lemon infused."

Infused? I had never been asked what kind of water I wanted. *It's water.*

"Lemon," I said with a small shrug.

I made my way to a small table in the corner and settled into the chair. If I was dressed in my usual homeless attire, I would feel super out of place. Everyone that walked in seemed to have some sort of preppy type of style. I glanced around once more and swallowed down the nervousness. I wondered if I was early or even in the right place. I reached in my purse for my phone, remembering that I had left it in the Jeep. Pushing the water away, I attempted to stand when a woman with steel-colored hair cut in a short bob stopped beside my table.

"Redhead?" she asked.

"Yes." I managed to answer.

The woman's ruby-red-lipped smile visibly faded as she looked me over. A moment of awkward silence passed as she looked through a black leather notebook.

"ID?" Her words were clipped with little emotion. I handed over my ID with a shaky hand, and she snatched it from my grasp. She scrutinized it and scribbled on the cream colored sheets before sliding it back over to me. Not once did she look at me, and I didn't know if that was a good sign or bad.

Clasping my hands in my lap, I leaned in a little. "Is something wrong?" I asked, my voice coming out mouse-like.

A line appeared between her brows. "I'll be honest with you," she said, closing the binder before locking her icy blue gaze on mine. "It's your size."

My belly became a sinking stone as her words seeped into my ears. I didn't need a billboard with my size and shape reminding me that I was on the curvier side. I knew girls in this business were typically on the smaller side, but I didn't think men would be that picky. Sex was sex at the end of the day.

"Listen, darling." Her tone softening ever so slightly. "I have no issue with large girls."

I almost winced at her words. I hated that term and preferred the word plus size or full-figured.

"But unfortunately, many men don't know what to do with this much *woman*, if you know what I mean." She waved her hands around before returning them to her lap.

I nodded, blinking hard.

"I think you're charming. But it's not up to me. The clients' tastes are what matter. I'm sorry."

Feeling the weight of the world on my shoulders, I stood and slid my arm through the strap of my purse. Fidgeting with my keys, I geared up to thank her for her time when she raised a finger to the air.

"Wait," she said as she locked her gaze on her phone screen.

Unsure of whether to sit or stand, I slowly lowered back into my seat and waited.

"I have a last minute client. He's not one of my regulars, but when he does book he usually spends a lot."

"You aren't going to give him to one of your more experienced girls?" I asked and then regretted it immediately because I needed this.

"They're all booked out for the weekend, and he asked for a real woman. Not a performer." She returned her gaze to meet mine. "His words, not mine."

"Okay. Thank you."

She handed me a thick business card. "There's a QR code on the back with a link to all the paperwork. Complete it no later than 11:59 tonight. Everything else you need to know will be texted afterward."

I took the card and thanked her again before heading back to my Jeep. Once inside, I leaned back into the torn seat and exhaled the breath I had been holding for the last few seconds. Gripping the steering wheel, I turned the Jeep over, and it sputtered to life. A wave of fear and relief washed over me as I pulled out of the parking space. For the first time in my life, I could honestly say things would get better.

CHAPTER 4
Hot Date ~ Carter

I HUNG up the phone and leaned back in my chair as I took a deep breath. It had been a hellish month at Castle Realty. We were booked out past the end of the year, yet my father, Christian Castle, kept taking on more clients. *You can never be too busy, son,* he always said. But, of course, these words usually came over the phone while he was sitting in a golf cart with a cocktail in hand. *If you're going to inherit my company, you need to prove you can handle being an entrepreneur.*

I looked around the room. I had a corner office at the top of the tallest building in Stonebridge. I leaned further back in my chair and twirled until my gaze locked on the Stonebridge skyline. I was apparently living the dream to the outside world, but I often found myself questioning my reasons for even wanting to inherit this. My grandfather and father worked hard to get the Castle name off the ground. Hard work and number crunching were in their blood, but it left their souls hollow and their hearts empty, with only the occasional cleaning staff and one night stand to occupy the halls of their homes and lives. I guess I couldn't complain much. My pay was great, and my employees were the best in the business, but the fact that I was the only heir to the "kingdom" made me the next in line by default, not by choice, and I hated not having choices, especially ones that dictated my career.

"Carter." His thunderous voice boomed into my office unexpectedly. Speak of the devil himself. "What are you still doing here, son?"

"Running your company," I said dryly. "Turns out it's a full-time gig."

His jaw tightened at my response, and I let my lips curl into a shit-eating grin. Nonchalantly pissing him off was something me and my younger brother prided ourselves in. We enjoyed letting our tongues lash out at his remarks. Unfortunately, my brother Finn took his hatred toward my father too far, and he sent him away. If my father had to hold on to anything with his last breath, it would always be his name, and it would have to be a cold day in hell before he let someone drag it through the mud. Family or not.

"Tell me you didn't forget about your date tonight," he said as he took a seat in one of the chairs sitting in front of my desk. His woodsy scent slammed into me like a riptide. The man practically bathed in it. I swallowed back a gag and raised a hand to my cheek.

"How could I forget?" I pinched the bridge of my nose. "You've been hooking me up on these 'dates' for months now."

His smile faded. "Carter, you are turning forty-four—"

"Forty actually, but go on." I drummed my finger on the desk.

He adjusted the lapels of his sports jacket. "You're single. Ever since Claire left you at the alter—"

"For your brother," I stated, cutting him off abruptly.

"You haven't even attempted to find a wife, and you know I want a grandchild before I die."

I stood up and slammed my laptop shut. "You mean, *grandson*. You want to die knowing you have a grandson to inherit Castle Realty."

I rounded the desk and walked toward the closet nestled in the corner of my office. I didn't have time to go home and change before the "date," but I figured I could at least change my shirt.

"Is it so bad that I want the legacy I built with my own sweat and blood to remain just that? A legacy?" He joined me in my closet and perched his ass on the corner of the large dresser. "You might actually like this girl. I chose a new agency for you. Word has it that these ladies love to please."

I tugged my shirt off, mumbling under my breath, hoping he didn't hear me. The last thing I needed was another lecture. I slipped into a black dress shirt, buttoning it before rolling the sleeves up a little.

"Is that what you're wearing?" He lifted a brow and folded his arms across his chest.

I ignored his jab at my attire and latched my watch around my wrist.

"All right, well, I'd wear a tie, but who am I to tell you what to do? Just try to act pleasant, will you? And don't talk about work too much. Women like it when you focus on them."

"Right," I said more or less through my teeth.

"I'm just trying to help, Carter."

"Yeah, well, I figure if I am paying for their time—"

He cut me off. "And pleasure…"

I resisted the urge to punch him. "I can talk about anything I damn well please."

"Sure, son. Whatever you have to do to give me a grandson."

With that, he walked out, and I glanced at my watch. The car was already parked in front when I made my way out of the building. I climbed into the back and gave my driver the address. The conversation with my father replayed in my head. My comment about paying for my date's time may have been over the top. But that's literally what it was. After so many failed dates, he lost faith in my ability to get a woman in my bed on my own terms and signed me up for an escort service. Most women were begging to take me to bed at the end of a date, and why wouldn't they? With strong builds, dark hair, olive skin, and a last name worth its weight in gold, we Castle men were like catnip to women who knew our name. But that also made dating unbearable most of the time. It was like being stuck between a rock and a hard place. I wanted to be with someone who wanted me for *me*. Not my name or money. Ironically my father wanted a grandson and didn't give a flying fuck about my feelings or the broken heart slowly dying in my chest.

ACCORDING TO MY FATHER, escorts were only escorting because of the easy money. He believed anyone dire enough to spread their legs for a few thousand dollars would be easily persuaded to give me a child for the right price. The whole thing was absurd. Disgusting really. But after forty years of having this man breathe down my neck, I was willing to do just about anything to get him to lay the fuck off.

I drifted my eyes back to the window as my car rode along at sloth speed. Traffic was a nightmare, and I looked down at my watch. "What's taking so long?" I barked out at my driver.

"Accidents," he said flatly.

"Can't you reroute?" I let out an annoyed huff and let my head fall against the headrest.

"I already have once. I'm sorry, Mr. Castle. Every road is backed up."

Fucking perfect. As much as I wasn't looking forward to this date, the last thing I wanted to do was reschedule. Fifteen minutes past the start time, my driver slowed as we approached the restaurant. Without stopping at the hostess station, I made my way toward the back, where a booth near the fireplace and the emergency exit was held on reserve for me all the time. Eyes followed me as I walked past the tables, and I bit back my annoyance. I couldn't go anywhere without people staring, and now I'm meeting an escort out in the open. Granted, I had no idea how this woman would look, and I hoped her outfit didn't scream I paid for sex. I told my father that if he was to continue setting me up with escorts, he should request a "real woman." I preferred the media and our colleagues not knowing about my father's shenanigans.

I ordered an Old Fashioned, took a generous sip, and let the bourbon calm my nerves. I was sweating, which meant I was nervous, which pissed me off. I wasn't the guy who got nervous around women, but something about this whole thing made me uneasy. Taking another sip, the liquor warmed my blood, and

I sat back and mulled over the conversation my father expected me to have with her before the end of the night. *Hi, I'm the heir to a massive real estate agency, and I need to secure a third in line before my father dies. Would you be willing to be my breeding vessel for a large sum of money?*

The realization of just how fucked I was made my lips curl, and I downed the last drops of my liquor. Returning my gaze to the front of the restaurant, I rested my eyes on a girl standing at the host stand. Her back was to my gaze, but that didn't stop my cock from taking note. I focused on her silk soft tresses and how they floated just below her shoulders. It was thick and wavy in an untamable way, but it wasn't her ringlets of silk spun hair that had my cock aching and my eyes glued to her. It was her dress and the highway of luscious curves that she concealed behind the deep colored fabric. I trailed my tongue across my bottom lip as I ate her up and noticed how short she was. I didn't know why but a tingle slithered down my spine as I thought about her raising her chin to meet my gaze as I towered over her.

She nodded at something the hostess was saying when she suddenly shifted her voluptuous body in my direction. She swept a lock of auburn colored hair behind her ear, and my heart slammed into my chest. My mouth watered as the realization slapped me in the face. A gold brooch in the shape of a heart nestled itself on the left side of her dress, and it was the signature symbol of the Creme de la Creme escort agency. But realizing that she was my escort wasn't why my breath hitched in my throat. The girl standing near the host stand was the same girl who served me my lunch the other day in the cafe. The hostess gave her a kind smile and led her toward my table. Almost forgetting my manners, I stood and extended my hand, motioning her to sit. Before she took the bait, her eyes shot up to meet mine, and she froze.

"Sit, please." I motioned to the opposite side of the black leather booth.

She paused, probably wondering if she should mention that we had contact before. She decided against it and forced the words lingering on her lips back down as she slid into the booth. I slid in simultaneously with her and locked our gaze once more. She had eyes that could only be described as mocha, a heart shaped face, and a pout begging to be invaded by my cock. I ignored the ache in my slacks and snatched the napkin from the table. *Fuck me.* Unsure of where to look, she settled her gaze on the glass of water as she bit the inside of her cheek. For a second, everything about this felt wrong, but the fog that had me second-guessing my actions soon faded when a light whimper flowed from her lips. The faint sound was enough to make my dick leak, and fuck did I want—*need*—to hear it again or so help me, God.

CHAPTER 5
Pretty Woman ~ Brooklyn

"CAN I GET YOU A DRINK, MISS?" the server asked.

I stiffened and searched the table for a drink menu, except there wasn't one. I tried to think, but it was hard with Carter's eyes peering into my soul. Heat coursed through my veins, and a chill ricocheted down my spine. I was sitting here in a fancy restaurant with the man I served a club sandwich to the other day. I wondered if he recognized me, and if he did, was he upset? Was he angry that he spent all this money on the girl from the cafe? *I'm officially a scammer.* The server cleared his throat, bringing me back to earth. I nodded, which wasn't exactly a response to the question.

"What would you like?" His brows creased as he looked down at me with annoyance.

A tiny wave of relief washed over me when the server placed a thick brown menu down in front of me. Daring not to look up at Carter, I paged through, pretending I knew what I was reading. Giving up, I closed it shut and met Carter's gaze, and his lips tipped into a smirk.

"What about a lemon drop?" he suggested as he pulled the drink menu from my grasp.

Not knowing what it was, I nodded and hoped it didn't taste bad or land me flat on my ass.

The server nodded and dismissed himself. Placing my hands in my lap, unsure of what to do or what to say, I rested my eyes on the highway of veins running under the skin of his hands.

"You'll like it," he insisted. "It's sugary."

Something about how he uttered that sentence made my heart skip in my chest. It seemed so innocent, yet dangerous at the same time. After meeting with the Madam yesterday, I went home and scanned the QR code. The online application took forever, and half of it I didn't understand. Blindly, I just submitted it all, and within minutes I got a confirmation email with all the information for the upcoming date. Other than Carter's name and age, I knew nothing. There wasn't even a photo. Maybe that was best, though, because I would have skipped town if he'd been an ogre.

I couldn't help the nausea that came over me after

that. It felt an awful lot like selling my soul—and body —to the devil. I called Mallory so I wouldn't throw up. As expected, she was excited. I think it was vicarious enthusiasm. The idea of all of this seemed to intrigue her.

After that, I went through the motions, going to work for a morning shift, running by the agency to pick up the gold peacock brooch that I was to wear on my dress, all before rushing back home to get ready.

Everything up until this moment had been a blur. And now, here I was, sitting in front of Carter Castle, the man who was paying for *me*, who also happened to be the sexy man from two days before that I couldn't stop my mind from wandering back to. How was this real life?

The server set our drinks down, and my eyes widened at the yellow liquid floating around the shallow martini glass. It had a sugar dipped rim with a lemon twist dangling off the edge. He was right; it did look good.

He took a sip of his dark liquor and pursed his lips together. "Are you ready to order?"

"Oh." Heat rushed to my cheeks once more as I glanced at the menu and then back at him.

I closed the menu and pushed it toward the edge of the table. "I think I'll take a Cesar salad."

"All our entrees come with salads," the server interrupted.

I offered a stiff smile. "I'm not very hungry," I lied. But I had no idea how to read this menu or what to order, and the last thing I needed was to add insult to injury as I struggled to pronounce the words of some exotic fish.

"I'll have the filet mignon, medium rare with the truffle butter," Carter said before snapping the heavy menu shut. "Also, the escargot."

Once we were alone again, I offered a small uncomfortable smile and took another sip of the delicious drink. It seemed a little sweeter than the first sip I took, and without thinking, I released a slow moan, and Carter's eyes narrowed as he took me in.

"You like that?" His words came out slow and lingered in the air around us.

I gulped and followed his movements, or rather the movement of his tongue, which slithered across his bottom lip in a swift motion.

"Are you sure you don't want more than that? You can literally have anything you want."

"I'm fine," I lied again.

He studied me before reaching for his cloth napkin and unfolding it on his lap. I copied his actions, assuming it was standard etiquette. In the process, though, I knocked one of my forks onto the floor, semi silencing the chatter around us. I didn't need a mirror to know that my face was the color of a tomato. He beat me to the punch before I could bend down to scoop it up. Crouching over, he grabbed it, and the small contact of his knuckle brushing against my ankle left a trail of fire on my skin. The server replaced the fork before setting a plate down in the center of our table. I stared at it, unsure of what I was looking at.

"Are those...snails?" I leaned in, peering at them with scrutiny.

He took another sip and winged a brow. "You've never had escargot before?"

I shook my head.

"Are there a lot of things you haven't done before?"

I toyed with my napkin as I dissected his question. Unsure of how to answer, I settled for watching him shift the small pair of tongs between his fingers before plucking it from the plate. Refusing to break our gaze, he gingerly pushed it past his lips and chewed. At that moment, I knew I lived under a rock because only I would need to fan the flames of my chest as I watched a grown man devour a snail. It seemed effortless as he repeated the process, then he handed over the tongs. My clumsiness shined through like the northern star, resulting in the snail flying across the room. Too embarrassed to see where it landed, I bowed my head into my palms and cringed inwardly.

Peeking my eyes through the slit of my fingers, I slowly lowered them. "I'm sorry, I—"

"It's fine. It just landed in that lady's hair. Don't

worry about it." He interjected as he raised his glass to his lips and winked.

"I don't ever do this," I admitted as I plucked at the cuticles of my fingers.

"No? I would have never guessed."

His words were dipped in sarcasm, but even so, I still deflated at the sheer embarrassment.

"I didn't mean to make fun of you. You're just so… fucking cute."

The way he said the words made my lips go from a pout to a tiny smile. His eyes lingered on my mouth, and he swallowed hard before clearing his throat.

"Here," he said, reaching for a piece of the toasted bread that bordered the plate. He dipped it in the sauce, which was green and buttery looking. "It's garlic butter and basil."

He lifted the bread to my mouth, and I looked at it, then at him.

"Don't be shy, baby girl." His words were low.

Baby girl?

I leaned in and took a bite from his hand while he used his other hand to touch my chin and tilt it up.

It's *delicious*.

Carter pulled his hand back, and I covered my mouth with a giggle as I chewed. "That's really good."

He sat back, watching me like some sort of prey that he wanted to devour as I patted the corners of my mouth with my napkin.

The rest of dinner went on, mostly with him asking me questions about myself as I tried not to knock anything else off the table.

The conversation shifted to his job, where I discovered he was the son of Christian Castle, a major real estate tycoon. My interest piqued.

"Meanwhile, Castle Realty will always be at the top of the industry. It still doesn't help what's going on with the market right now," he said before pausing to sip his drink.

I swallowed down the bite of my salad and licked the dressing from the corner of my mouth. "Because sales are bottlenecking?"

"Right..." His words trailed off as his brows stitched together. "How did you know that?"

I stabbed my fork into the salad and sliced my eyes to the plate. "I am taking night classes for business, and I've been interested in real estate lately."

He forked a piece of his steak and paused. "Really?"

"I mean, I don't know much," I protested.

"Sounds like you know a lot more than most people." He winked and then pushed the juicy meat between his lips.

Butterflies were taking over my stomach, and I felt like a little school girl sitting across from this man. Every wink, smirk, and hand movement had my breath hitching in my throat, and as each second passed, the need to hold my thighs together increased. Taking the last bite of his steak, he shoved his plate to the side and folded his arms across his chest. I wondered if I somehow was under scrutiny with the intensity of his gaze, and then his words left me breathless.

"Um...What?" I fumbled the words off my lips.

I had never seen a man smile so much before I met Carter, but it wasn't just any type of smile. It was salacious, dangerous, and hungry.

"'How much do you weigh?" He repeated.

I tilted my head to the side and then gave him a slightly off number, about twenty pounds off. He traced a thumb across his lip, and the slits around his eyes tightened. Did he know I was lying?

He eased in, pressing his hard chest to the wide table, and held up his finger. "Don't lie to me, baby girl. I'm only asking because I want you to ride my face. The heavier, the better."

The server returned and snapped up his empty glass before replacing it with a new one. Carter held my gaze, and I shrank. I never sat on anyone before, let alone someone's face, but the thought of doing it to him intrigued me but also frightened me. I took another careful sip of my drink and contemplated finishing it off, because I had no idea what he had in store for the rest of the evening.

"You know, I was a little nervous about tonight. But

now that I've seen you, I'm really looking forward to what our evening has to offer," he said as he tipped the rim of the glass to his lips.

Shit. Guess I'm sitting on his face.

After dinner, we made our way outside. Carter's hand rested on my lower back, right above my butt, as he guided me out of the restaurant. A black SUV with tinted windows idled near the curb, and Carter reached in front of me to open up the passenger side door. An earthy yet masculine scent clinched around my lungs, and I climbed into the SUV. He followed in behind me, and at that moment, I realized just how big he was. His thighs resembled tree trunks as he rested one against mine, and a smile pulled at the corners of my lips. I always tried to make myself smaller next to men, and this was the first time that I felt smaller in comparison. He motioned to the driver, and I nestled into the leather seat. After a few minutes, I noticed that we were headed in the wrong direction of my house.

"My house is that way," I broke the silence awkwardly.

Carter cut his gaze in my direction. "We're going to a hotel," he said softly.

Oh. Right. A hotel. Because I'm an escort, and this is a business transaction. I returned my attention to the window and did everything to keep the salad and bread from bubbling in my stomach.

CHAPTER 6
Sweet Temptation ~ Carter

IF I HAD TO GUESS, Brooklyn was a virgin, and if she wasn't, her experience was limited. The thought of her stealing my last breath with her luscious bubble butt had my flesh begging to be let out. I had to shift numerous times during dinner, and every time her cheeks turned a shade darker, my wall weakened. I dated many women over the past decade or two, and never have I ever felt the need to protect them. A rouge wave slapped me in the face when she turned and locked eyes with me in the cafe two days ago, and now that I had her in my grasp, letting her go seemed insane. I glanced in her direction, taking in the streaks of auburn locks that the sun naturally lightened. Her big brown eyes scanned the neighborhood as we rode past luxury shops and cute coffee cafes. Her preoccupied state allowed me to run my eyes over every inch of her curves at my leisure. *Fuck.* Although the cabin was cloaked in silence, my thoughts were anything but. The tension in my muscles, paired with the strain in my pants, was the perfect recipe for combustion. I wondered if she kept her attention toward the window because she could feel my eyes on her. I wanted her to feel it. Fuck, I wanted her to feel a lot of things. My tongue for one, and then my cock molding to her walls as I stretched her out.

"How old are you?" I asked, breaking the silence.

Her eyes snapped over to me, allowing me to catch a whiff of the fading scents of her floral perfume. I recognized it immediately, and I also knew she didn't make enough to afford it. She tucked a lock of hair behind her ear. "Twenty-one."

"Perfect."

Of course, she was over eighteen, but knowing that she was freshly legal made a tingle zip down my spine. She was old enough to drink, old enough to fuck, and old enough to breed. We pulled into the hotel porte-cochere, and her mouth fell open. Her sea glass eyes widened as she took in the sights. The entire ordeal had me relaxing in the seat as she looked around. So fucking innocent. How could I let her go? The bellhop opened the passenger door, and we climbed out. With her eyes fixated on the large golden doors in front of her, she didn't notice the summer breeze had her cocktail dress lifting in a Marilyn-

Esque swoop. My gaze locked on her white teddy bear-dotted panties by the time her hands struggled against the wind.

Fuck me.

I motioned her toward the doors, I placed my hand on the small of her back just low enough to feel the slope of her ass. A giddiness seemed to sweep over her, and she appeared to drown in the luxury as I guided her to the elevator banks. Her eyes sliced from the crystal chandeliers down to the oriental rugs and the large leather furniture. There were over a dozen hotels in Stonebridge, but only one Pinnacle. Castle men enjoyed decadent food, strong liquor, and upscale accommodations.

"Sorry," she said, looking up at me. "There's just so much I've never experienced in the world."

I ran a knuckle down the softness of her cheek and tucked a lock of hair behind her ear. She ignored my actions as she tilted her chin toward the ceiling. She had no idea how many new experiences she was about to have. I found myself mentally comparing our worlds. She had limited life experiences and funds from the look of it. As we made our way through the lobby, she spun in a circle and slightly toppled as she bumped into the elevator wall.

"Have you ever seen anything so wonderful?" She beamed with the eagerness of a child.

I couldn't stop the smile that tugged at my lips. "I haven't," I said, but I wasn't talking about the hotel.

The ride to the top floor took less than a minute, and the elevator doors peeled back. Taking her hand, I guided her down the quiet hallway. Scanning the platinum keycard over the reader, I pushed the door open with a light nudge and motioned her inside. The whites of her eyes brightened as she looked around and seeing her experience something so normal to me made my heart thump in my chest.

"I could fit my entire apartment in this space alone," she said as she sauntered over to the balcony.

I stepped out of my shoes and plucked at the top button of my dress shirt. The minibar called to me, and I poured myself a stiff drink to lessen the blow of the ache that refused to subside. Her innocent reactions just made my cock harder, and my eyes settled on the hem of her dress, which rode up a few inches as she peered over the balcony. Emotions that I buried years ago started to rush to the surface as I held her in my sight. Torn between wanting to protect her and keep her safe and wanting to fill her little cunt up with my seed. I finished off my drink and poured another, this one was for her, and I made sure to go heavy on the Bordeaux cherry syrup. The high of her new adventure was wearing off, and she slipped back inside with slumped shoulders, and fell into the softness of the couch. Refusing to look up at me as I approached, I lowered the drink to her hands.

"I wish I could stay in this moment forever," she whispered.

My heart dropped through a trapdoor in my stomach when her words flowed off her tongue. Maybe this was my cue to tell her that I planned on keeping her forever. She was dreading what came next. I didn't want that. I wanted her to want me as much as I wanted her.

"Here." I rocked the glass back and forth in front of her.

"Thanks."

Fuck. Her timidity was so sexy.

I clinked my glass against hers, and she took a reluctant sip and winced.

"Sorry. I tried to sweeten it up for you." A lopsided grin tugged at the corner of my mouth, and I raised my glass back to my lips.

"Can't hide turpentine under sugar," she said as a cough erupted from her throat.

I nearly spat my drink out at her snarkiness and almost busted my load in my pants. *Jesus Christ.*

I took her drink and set it on the side table before lowering to my knees. Pushing my way between her honey-thick thighs, she let out a soft whine, and it nearly killed me.

"Look at me," I told her, my voice low but direct. "I want you to look into my eyes when we talk, okay?"

She nodded obediently, and I clipped a finger under her chin. She pulled her bottom lip between her teeth, and a bolt of desire shot through me as I watched it slip back out slowly.

"I know you're nervous, baby girl, but I won't make you do anything you're not ready for. Not yet anyway, but..." I let my words trail off and eyed her movements. "But I need two things from you before the night ends." I rose and looked down at her.

She followed my gaze, her neck reminded me of a crane, and I rested my eyes on the ridges of her throat.

"Um, okay?"

My hand found her cheek, and I let my finger glide across her warm skin. "I want you. I want to keep you, love you and fuck you, in that order. Do you want me to?"

I waited with bated breath for her answer, but all she could do was swallow. Her lips parted and closed, uncertainty filling her brain. She teased me, and she didn't even know it. Her words turned to mush as she tried to formulate a coherent sentence, but it was useless. So made her feel instead. The room stilled, and I forced my tongue between her lips. She melted, then whimpered, and the pads of her fingers found the waistband of my pants. We played tug of war for a few seconds, and every time she tried to pull away, I just deepened the kiss. I stole one breath after the other and growled at the sound of her gasp when I broke our kiss. Swollen wet lips looked good on her, and I'm dying to know how the other pair tasted.

"Well? Do you want me?" I asked as I rested my forehead against hers.

Her eyes fluttered, and she nodded. Overwhelmed and flustered, I tilted her chin and forced her gaze to mine.

"Perfect. Now, will you be a good girl and ride my fucking face?"

She studied me, consuming the hunger in my eyes, and for a moment, I was sure she was gonna change her mind until she gave me the answer I wanted to hear. I pulled her from the couch and tugged her toward the master bedroom before she could change her mind. We passed the king-size bed, and I walked into the bathroom.

I took a step back. "I'll let you freshen up a little bit, but don't take too long, or I'll knock this damn door down."

I closed the door and got rid of every ounce of clothing except my boxers. As badly as I needed a release, fucking her wasn't in the cards tonight, and releasing the beast would only tempt me to take her. I settled on the bed and waited. Counting seconds under my breath, I listened as she turned on the faucet. I meant what I said about her not taking too long. I wanted to *taste her*, not soap. The bathroom door opened, and she sauntered out. Her purple cocktail dress still covered her beautiful curves. I raised a brow and shook my head. Biting the inside of her cheek, she slowly lowered the dress and let it drop to the floor. She stood frozen in her pink bra with teddy bear dotted panties. I crooked a finger, and she rushed over. She was no escort, far from it. She was a baby girl in a bad situation and needed to be saved. *Thank fuck I was her hero.*

"I've never done this—"

"You are fucking beautiful, and daddy's going to devour you," I said, interrupting her. "Here." I patted my lap.

She climbed onto the bed and then stopped out of confusion. "Um…"

"Face me." I took her hand and guided her body toward my body.

She planted one leg on either side of me and lowered her juicy ass to my chest. I removed the pillow that propped my head and wrapped my hands around her waist.

She placed her arms in front of her stomach. "Do you want me to remove my panties?" Her words came out in a whisper, and I couldn't help but chuckle.

"No," I said before gliding my tongue across my bottom lip.

Her panties were thin, and my tongue could easily

please her through the fabric, but I didn't want to ask her to remove them. I wanted her to do it all on her own.

"Closer…" I cooed.

She scooted closer, and when only an inch remained between my lips and the crotch of her panties, I pulled her forward. My abrupt actions almost made her lose her balance, but I firmly placed my hands on her hips and ground her in place. With an unyielding gaze, I studied her. The fact that she tried to hide her emotions only made me devour her harder. The thin fabric was no match for my tongue. I teased her for a few minutes, purposely sliding my tongue around the clit. She squirmed, then whimpered, and I waited.

"Please, can you—"

I lifted her off my mouth. "Can I what?" I raised my lips to her crotch and teased her. "Use your words, baby. Can I what?"

"Make me come." The words fell off her lips.

My body throbbed for her, and I pushed the crotch of her panties to the side, exposing plump pussy lips. I dragged my tongue between her folds and then circled the clit. Her flesh tingled at the contact, and I latched my lips around the swollen bud. She unraveled as the seconds passed, and her light whimpers turned into moans. My grip on her waist tightened, and I held her in place as her orgasm quickly approached. Her mouth fell open, and I couldn't help slip my thumb past her luscious lips. A wave of desire hit me like a ton of bricks when her body went into spasms sending a wave of tingles down my spine. I detached my lips to let out an ear-shattering "fuck" as I came like a schoolboy in my boxers. I lifted her off my chest and placed her down next to me. Her eyes hooded, and I had to hold myself back from forcing myself between her thighs. I tangled my fingers in her thick tresses and gave her a soft tug to steal her attention.

"Where are you from?" I asked.

"South of here," she said, her voice breathy as her fingertips brushed over my chest.

"Do you have any siblings?"

"An older brother," she said, bringing her hand up to trace the large decorative tattoo that stretched across my chest.

I let her get lost in the artwork as her dainty fingers sent a wave of fire through my veins. My father hated them, and that's why Finn and I got them. It was the one thing that allowed us to express our feelings and piss our father off simultaneously.

"Is this a broken heart?" she asked in reference to the blackened heart ripped in half on the left side of my chest.

I nodded and pulled her into my grasp before she started asking questions I didn't feel like answering. My last relationship ended five years ago, and although time seemed to fly by as the days went on, the splinter that pierced my heart remained. A constant reminder that heartache was lingering around the corner.

"Why are you doing this?" I asked.

Her eyes darted up to mine, and the warmth that stirred behind her warm chocolate eyes evaporated, leaving sadness behind, and I hated myself instantly.

She didn't answer me. She just looked down and picked at the plush fabric of the duvet.

"Brooklyn?" I demanded.

Not sure if it was the bass in my voice, but when she finally yielded to my gaze, her Bambi-like eyes were brimmed with tears.

I cupped her cheek in the palm of my hand and let my thumb graze across it just as a tear began to fall.

CHAPTER 7
Bound to Breed - Brooklyn

CARTER ASKED for the third time why I decided to sleep with him for money, and I eventually gave in to his request. I told him everything, from my foster childhood to Lincoln's most recent arrest. When I finished spilling the beans of my shit life, I felt exhausted, exposed, and ashamed. I spent the past half hour digging up every traumatic experience that held me together and laid it out for a complete stranger to digest, *a super hot and sexy stranger, but a stranger.* I lowered my eyes to the duvet and waited for the tears to cascade over my lashes. The bed dipped as he stood and walked over to the floor-to-ceiling windows overlooking the hotel garden. The air stilled, and he let his shoulders rise and then fall as a heavy sigh dripped off his lips. I wondered what he was thinking? Feeling? Did my sad life story really dampen the mood? His attention turned back toward me, and he sauntered across the room. I tugged at the duvet, pulling it up to my eyes as he removed his boxers and tossed them in the trash can near the bathroom door. I wondered if he had come when he yelled my name along with a string of curse words as he lifted me off his mouth.

He left the master bedroom, but only for a second before returning with his phone in hand. Walking over to my side of the bed, he lowered himself and my eyes locked on the monstrous flesh commanding my attention. He scrolled through the apps, and my mind went into a frenzy when he pressed the gold and black icon. *Crap.* I shouldn't have talked about my personal life. I should have brushed it off and kept it professional. He typed in a few things before setting the phone on the nightstand. I bit the inside of my cheek and wracked my brain for some sort of apology for ruining the mood when I heard my phone buzz. He nudged me to grab it, and when my eyes locked on the screen, my chest bottomed out. *Contract with Carter Castle extended and locked for 10 months.*

I looked up at him, surprised at the soft expression on his otherwise hard and chiseled face.

"I don't understand," I stuttered.

His eyes shifted from their softer state, and hunger revived them as he held my gaze.

"You need money, and I've got money. As a matter

of fact, check your bank account. I made the first direct deposit."

"First?" I asked as I thumbed through the apps on my home screen. My mouth dropped open at the $5,955 staring back at me. *Fucking forty-five dollar overdraft fee.* "Why are you doing this for me? This couldn't be because you feel sorry for me."

His stare penetrated my soul. "Because I need a child. An heir and you are going to give me an heir."

I sat there for a minute, my head dizzy with all of this. The money. The suggestion. I mean, it's not really a suggestion. The contract was initiated. Carter Castle wanted to get me pregnant, and he was willing to pay. I needed the money. That was a no brainer, but did I really want to go through this? Ten months was a long time to spend with someone I was attracted to but had no desire to be with me in the long run.

I sat up; the chilled air wrapped around me and shivered down my spine. "Is this why you asked me if I was attracted to you? Because you wanted to breed me?"

"Nope." He popped the "p" and stood. "I asked if you were attracted to me because I plan on keeping you forever," he said as he eased in to stroke a finger across my cheek.

"Then why the contract?"

He placed his back in my direct line of sight and walked to the door, stopping just before passing the threshold that separated the bedroom from the rest of the suite.

"So you'll stay. I'm a busy man, and trust me, baby girl, you don't want me to chase after you. I always find what's mine."

"Oh…" I let my words trail off as I digest his promise.

He winked. "Get dressed. It's late. I'll have my driver take you home, and I'll talk to you first thing tomorrow."

"I can get an Uber its—"

"Over my dead body. You're my little girl now, and daddy said you're taking the car." He yelled from the other room.

I slumped back into the soft pillows and gazed up at the cathedral ceiling. I had no idea what I was supposed to be feeling now, but at least the worry of money was no longer weighing me down.

CHAPTER 8
Sealing the Deal~Carter

I GOT to the office the next morning before the sun rose, which wasn't unusual for me, but today was different. I was getting ready for my time away. A small part of me wilted when she told me about her past and the problems with her brother. The protector in me wanted to wipe away all her worries and tell her everything would be okay, but I knew she wouldn't take my words at face value. Although life dealt her a shit card, she had her wits about her, and I admired that. She had every opportunity to go down the wrong path, yet she stayed the course. The moment I laid eyes on her again in the restaurant, I knew I couldn't let her go, and as the minutes chipped away, the further the night went on, I was left with two options. Bound her to a contract she couldn't resist or kidnap her and tie her to my bed in a mansion on a remote island. Ironically, the thought of bringing a kid into my superficial, shallow world bothered me, and it wouldn't be the end of the world if she didn't get pregnant, but I would be lying to myself if I said I didn't find utter joy in filling her sweet cunt up with my cream.

Once she left me last night, I opened my special tracker app to watch the green dot move along the Stonebridge streets. I installed it while she was cleaning up in the bathroom. She left her phone unlocked, and I took that as my opportunity. I trusted her, but still, having her exact location at my fingertips calmed the fire that burned my nerves. Every muscle in my body tensed as my car crept closer to South Shore. I feared for her life in that part of Stonebridge. I decided last night, after I beat my dick repeatedly to the memory of her beautiful facial features, that I wanted her to live with me for the next ten months. She stumbled to give me an answer, but a reluctant "yes" seeped into my ear, which was the only answer I needed.

I packed up the most important things in a few small boxes. I had my assistant put any meetings that weren't urgent on hold for the rest of the day, and since my father was on a golf vacation in Florida, he wouldn't notice my absence from the office for a few days. The day passed swiftly, and once 4:30 p.m. rolled around, I booked it for the elevator to find my car waiting for me. I didn't even remember the last time I left the office when the sun was still shining. My eight-hour workdays had quickly became twelve-hour workdays as I buried myself into the business and ignored everything else, but ignoring Brooklyn wasn't an option. The ride to her apartment didn't take long, and the car slowed, pulling up to a brick two-story building. My jaw tightened as I took in the nightmare that she called home. Someone could easily break in and do God knows what to her. Any uncertainty that lingered about my decision to have her come live with me evaporated as I scanned the surroundings. There was no way in hell I could leave someone as precious as her here. The driver sounded the horn, garnering the attention of the flock of thugs hanging on the corner in the distance. She appeared in the doorway with the strap of a heavy duffle digging into her shoulder. The sun settled on her luscious plump figure as she made her way toward the car, and I wanted to eat her. Ripped jeans covered her legs, and her soft belly peeked from under a purple crop top with an animated avocado on it. Despite being dressed down, my jeans grew tight at the sight of her, and suddenly wetness coated the top of my boxers. *Fuck.*

As she approached the car, my driver got out to attend to the trunk, and I opened the passenger door. A sudden cat call stopped all three of us in our tracks.

Those same low-life thugs were smoking cigarettes with their eyes locked on my baby girl with gritty smiles.

"How about that ride, sugar?" One of them called out.

An intense throb occupied the back of my jaw as I clenched down on my molars. I locked my eyes on them and drew in a deep breath. I grabbed her duffle and handed it to my driver. The trunk slammed shut, and I let out a breath as I motioned her to get inside. "Your chariot awaits, little girl."

She froze, and my pulse skittered with negative anticipation, then her eyes crinkled with a smile. I rolled my eyes and let a smile tear at my lips as she mocked me with the cutest fucking curtsey before climbing into the car.

The ride back to my house didn't take long. She kept her eyes on the window the entire time, and I kept my hand on her thigh. I let her use the time to sort through her thoughts. Asking someone to have your kid wasn't a small favor, no matter how big the price tag attached to the question. The only thing I wanted to do was calm her mind and make her feel secure.

"I didn't even know this part of Stonebridge existed," she said, breaking the silence for the first time.

"There are many things in the world you have yet to indulge in, baby doll. But don't worry. I'll see to it that you experience everything..." I slipped my fingers inside one of the holes in her jeans and brushed her velvety soft skin.

She tensed, and a tiny squeak of a giggle bubbled up from her throat as she bit back a laugh. She's ticklish. *Well, that's going to be fun.* The car slowed as it approached a large black gate.

"This is your house?" The whites of her eyes brightened as she looked around.

"One of them," I answered.

I loved watching her mouth pop open like that. Her full lips round with awe. It made my dick pulse, and shamelessly, I adjusted myself. She became paralyzed at the grandeur of her new home, and I grinned, loving that it had that effect on her. I took her hand, pulling her to the front door.

We stepped inside, and I closed the door behind us. Brooklyn stopped, accidentally dropping her things as she took in the entrance.

She bent down with flushed cheeks, and a soft "oops" rolled off her lips.

"I'm sorry. I've only been here for thirty seconds, and I'm already making a mess in your home."

I crouched down next to her, covering her small hand with mine. "First of all, never apologize for anything again. Do you hear me?"

She nodded. "Yes, sir."

"Daddy," I corrected.

She blinked. "What?"

"Don't call me sir. It's not, sir. Or Mr. Castle. You can call me Carter. But I'd prefer you call me daddy."

She swallowed and nodded.

"Also, this is your home now, too. I've labeled all the cabinets so you know where everything is. You have an entire closet to yourself. Every inch of it is yours."

"Yes sir—I mean...*Daddy*..."

The word came out in a hesitant whisper so soft it might as well have been a prayer. My skin pricked in goose bumps at the sound. Jesus, hearing her say it like that was enough to end me right here. She had absolutely no idea how much power she had over me, and I couldn't wait to hear her desperate cry as her fingernails scraped my back while I pounded her sweet little pussy.

I helped her gather the rest of her things off the floor and slowly ran my fingers over each item. Bubblegum. Headphones. Strawberry lip balm and Tampons. *Once I'm done filling her up, she won't be needing those.* The last thing that caught my eye was her keys, and I snatched them up before she had a chance to.

"I'll take care of your apartment," I said as I rose.

"Oh, well, the lease is—"

"Baby girl..." I let my words trail off and raised a

brow. A gentle reminder that she didn't need to worry anymore. Daddy was here.

She tucked a thick strand of hair behind her ear and tipped the left toe of her sneaker inward. Oh yes, I was certain she had no idea how she made me feel. I took a step forward, removing the space between us, and pulled her into my grasp. Hints of her lip balm seeped onto my tongue as I deepened our kiss, and her hands pulled on the lapel of my sports jacket as she rose to her tippy toes.

I stubbornly broke our kiss and rested my forehead against hers. "Hungry?"

She wrinkled her little button nose and peered over my shoulder.

"It smells yummy."

"Good, because I had my chef make something you might enjoy." I placed a soft kiss on her forehead and pulled her in the direction of the kitchen. I never had dinner made and usually ate out before heading home, but I wanted to make her first night here special. I contacted my old friend Aiden, who owned a private security firm in Stonebridge. I had him run a soft background check on Brooklyn and paid him a little extra to do some light-hearted digging. He emailed me an encrypted file around noon with everything he thought I wanted to know. Now I knew that she liked sweets, French bulldogs, the show *Bridgerton* and had good taste in food, her favorite being home-style penne pasta.

We stepped into the kitchen, and I rounded the center island to grab a bottle of wine and two glasses. She joined me and plopped down on the wooden stool next to me. I loved how her crop top rose slightly as she leaned into the island. The waistband of her jeans rolled down, exposing her soft muffin top. She caught my gaze and tugged on her shirt, but I stopped her.

"Don't you dare." I let the fabric slowly slip from my grip and rose my hand to stroke a finger down her cheek. "I hope you like Merlot."

I slid the glass toward her, and she picked it up. A low hum vibrated off her chest, and I pulled her from the stool she was sitting on and into my lap. Confused at first, she tried to pull away, but my grip around her waist was stronger.

"I don't want to crush you," she said as she lifted her chin to peer up at me.

"That's not physically possible."

Refusing to let her out of my grasp, I assembled our penne pasta into a large bowl and topped it off with parmesan dusting. Holding up two forks, she took one and tipped it into the pasta.

"Do you always share your meals with hookers?" She joked and stabbed her fork into the pasta.

I tightened my grip around her waist and nudged my lips against the shell of her ear. "Keep being a brat, and I'll put you over my knee." I pulled her earlobe between my teeth and let it slip out slowly. "Also, I haven't shared my life with anyone in over five years, and don't ever degrade yourself while in my presence. Understood?"

My tone was clipped, but I needed her to understand that she was more to me than some escort. She was my baby girl, and she was all mine. We continued our dinner and conversed over our past life experiences, our likes, dislikes, and favorite things. We had so much in common yet came from extremely different backgrounds. Our conversations only solidified my decision.

"What did you do today?" I asked as I took a sip of wine.

"I had a short shift at Estelle's. Then I just worked on getting ahead on my homework."

"Good girl. Daddy loves time management."

My words made her cheeks turn a shade of pink, and I wondered if they also made her wet.

I lifted her off my lap as I stood and pressed my chest into her, trapping her. Her breathing picked up, and I lifted her onto the island in one swift movement. With each of my arms on either side of her, she licked her lips and dropped her eyes to the floor.

I clipped a finger under her chin and eased in. "I do need one more thing from you." I traced a thumb over her bottom lip. "I need you to quit your job."

"What? Why?" she asked.

I ran my hands up her luscious thighs and parted them. "Because the only job you'll have now is going to school, taking long baths, and letting daddy fill you to the brim with his seed. So, are you going to be a good girl for me?"

CHAPTER 9
*Bathe Me, Choke Me, F*ck Me ~ Brooklyn*

CARTER'S WORDS made my nerves feel like live wires. His affection toward me was a lot to process, mainly because I had never felt these emotions before, but one thing was certain, I loved the way he made me feel. He took all my worries and lifted them off my shoulders like they weighed nothing, and the more I thought about it, the more I had to control my breathing. He forced his way between my legs and poured us another glass of wine. We sipped it in silence, and as I tried to find something to rest my gaze upon, his eyes devoured me. A shiver skipped down my spine as I watched him sipped his wine. His words and actions so far were laced with kindness and care, but tonight I wouldn't be going home, which meant he had all night to ravish my body. It scared me but also excited me. I couldn't help the anticipation in my stomach. It trailed down lower, the thought of his hands on me making me involuntarily wet. I squeezed my thighs together, forgetting that his massive frame was separating them for a slight moment. When a sinister smirk crawled across his lips, I sliced my gaze away and tossed back the rest of my wine.

"Gearing up?"

I nodded and then quickly shook my head. He finished his wine, and my eyes pinned on the bob of his Adam's apple.

"You're so fucking cute. You can gear up all you want. Please do whatever you need to do. I don't mind, but just know I'll be taking all your holes, and you can't run." He lifted me off the counter and took my empty wine glass. "Well, you could. I don't mind the chase."

I twirled a loose strand of hair around my finger and lied. "I wasn't gearing up."

"Right." He winked and loaded the glasses into the dishwasher. "It's bath time, baby."

"I usually just take showers before bed."

He tilted his chin, and a deep growl vibrated off his chest.

Heat crept into my cheeks, and I looked down like a puppy who's been swatted with a newspaper.

We walked out of the kitchen, and he led me through the maze of his home, stopping at a small flight of stairs in front of a large French door. He pushed it open, and my mouth fell to the floor. Somehow I believed he liked seeing me in awe and did it on purpose. We rounded the corner of his master bedroom and walked into his master bath. Of course, like the rest of his life, it was grand, so much so that I was afraid to touch anything.

"Can anyone see in? It feels very...open," I said as I looked out the windows.

His usual smirk appeared as he bent over the large black clawfoot tub and turned on the water. "No."

The rustling of a cream-colored bag caught my attention. I strained my neck and watched as he retrieved a large bottle of fancy bubble bath. He gave a quick wink and then unscrewed the top. It smelled divined as it melted into the warm water. A seductive mixture of ginger, lemon, and vanilla coated the air, and my spine nearly liquefied. I clenched my teeth when he peeled off his shirt and tossed it into the hamper. I didn't think I would ever get used to seeing the wall of abs chiseled into his chest.

"I have no neighbors behind me, so you don't have to worry about anyone but me seeing your beautiful naked body," he said as he took two long strides, closing the space between us.

His tucked his fingertips beneath the hem of my shirt, grazing my skin. "Don't be shy, little girl," he said in a gritty tone. "Daddy would never hurt you."

I didn't know whether his words calmed me or

made me even more nervous. But I knew his touch, the intensity in his eyes, and the fact that he smelled like amber and spice made my nipples hard.

He noticed, of course, and stepped closer until his crotch pressed against my navel. I blinked, and then my shirt was no longer covering my body, and I blinked again to find that my breasts had bounced down once he unclasped my bra. I covered myself and rested my arms in front of my belly out of habit. Still to this day, past experiences scarred me, but the rigid rise and fall in Carter's chest as he took me in told me that he was more than capable of handling me.

"Do you like when I touch you?"

I nodded and chewed on my bottom lip.

"Use your words."

"I like it when you…I mean, daddy touches me."

He let his finger trail down the side of my face until his thumb brushed along the column of my throat, then he gripped it as he dragged his tongue across his bottom lip. All the air deserted my lungs, but the feeling between my legs really stole my breath.

His fingers trailed down my neck to my collar bone. He ran his thumb along my throat, gripping it momentarily as he dragged his bottom lip through his teeth. "I can tell," he said, his eyes on my chest. My nipples could cut glass.

He took a step back and lowered his lips to my neck, slowly making his way between my breasts as he descended. His lips met the waistband of my jeans, and his hands worked their magic to pull them down. He made sure to take my panties too. I stepped out, feeling overly self-conscious. I anticipated his tongue dragging across my folds, but he grinned instead as he rose to his feet. The loss of the possibility of contact made me swell. It physically hurt.

"How hot do you like it?" he asked, walking back by the tub.

"What?" I choked out.

He looked back at me. "The water?" A grin crawled across his face. "What did you think I meant?"

My face was burning. "I...I don't..." I cleared my throat.

He released a lighthearted chuckle and gestured me to the tub. Taking my hand, he helped me step in, and I lowered myself into the water. It burned, but it felt perfect. Mountains of bubbles continued to rise as water rushed out of the faucet, and I couldn't help but blow a few that floated up. Keeping his eyes on me, he walked back over to the vanity where the bag was sitting and pulled a few items from it. I leaned forward to see a few rubber ducks tucked under his arm. He tossed them in, one at a time, and each splash coated my face with bubbles.

"They're floating away," he said as he eyed the pink and purple ducks.

I stretched my arms and yanked them toward me,

struggling to get them in a little straight line. The water splashed once more, and this time my eyes locked on a colorful ball bobbing up and down. I grabbed it without being told and attempted to get all the toys in a neat fashion. I didn't know how many minutes passed before I looked back up in his direction, but once I did, he was kneeling behind me with his arms on either side of the tub.

"Does baby girl like her bath toys?"

I nodded, and he placed a kiss on my head. Being an adult and playing in a bubble bath with toys was an odd feeling, but I enjoyed it. It calmed me and made me feel safe and protected. Vulnerability was never an option for me, but Carter changed that the more time we spent together.

He tugged my head back and lifted the sprayer hanging off the edge of the tub. "What are their names?"

"They don't have names." My voice came out much higher than expected, and I shrank back down a little.

"Can you name them for daddy?" he asked as he tilted my head back further.

Warm water soaked my scalp, followed by a citrus smelling shampoo. I gathered up the ducks and bopped each one on the beak with my finger.

"The purple one name is fuzzy muffin, the pink one name is cotton candy, and the chocolate one name is coco."

"Good girl. Tilt your head for daddy."

I leaned back and closed my eyes as his hands massaged my scalp. The feeling pushed a light moan from my lips, and he responded with a soft growl. I took pleasure in knowing I could turn him on, although sometimes I wondered how someone so attractive and of such high status could be turned on by me.

"Mmm, you like that princess?" he asked, interrupting my wild thoughts.

I nodded. "It feels so good."

"You have no idea how good daddy is going to make you feel, baby girl."

Before I could open my eyes to look at him, he ran his hands down my chest. His movements were soft and intentional as he traced the outline of my full breasts before his fingertips circled my nipples.

"Daddy wants to hear you fucking moan," he whispered into my ear.

I hesitated and then did as told.

With his hands still on my hips, he lowered his lips to mine and let his tongue run along my lips before parting them. His kiss was greedy, possessive, and mind-blowing.

Breaking the spellbound kiss, he moved his lips to the shell of my ear. "Spread those fucking legs for daddy," he whispered.

I hesitated at first and then obliged.

His grip on my wet tresses tightened as he pulled my head back, and his other hand found my throat. Trapped in his grip, I arched my back, exposing my breasts to the cool air, and it pebbled my nipples. He choked me just enough to make my breath grow thin and then released me as a gasp floated on my tongue. He did it repeatedly, and every second, my heart slammed in my chest, and my clit throbbed. My chest fell when he allowed me to breathe and rose when he enjoyed watching me struggle. The mixture of warm water and cold air circled my raw nipples, making a shard of ice skip down my spine, and I craved it. Once he released his hand, my lungs swelled with air, and his hand crept down to my folds. He teased me and made delicate circles around my clit. *God, does this man know what he's doing.*

I arched my back again, my breasts surfacing from the water, in hopes he would touch them again. I needed every sensation. He knew what I wanted, but he didn't use his hand. Instead, he lowered his head, closing his mouth around one of my nipples.

I gripped the edges of the tub, and he picked up the pace. "Daddy."

He worked my clit with his fingers and nearly brought me to the edge before pulling away. I whimpered, and a devilish grin spread across his face as he looked down at me. The pads of his fingers paused over my lips, and I opened for them.

"Ready to take my cock, princess?"

I stepped out of the tub with his help, and he wrapped a warm towel around me. I looked at it more carefully, realizing it was dotted with tiny teddy bears.

"I bought it for you," he said. "It looked like something you'd like."

"It's cute."

That made his eyes lighter and his smile almost playful. "You're cute."

We made our way to the bedroom. It was connected directly to the bathroom, with no doors. There's a mix of stone and wood walls with what looks like a California king size platform bed. It looked both manly and comfy at the same time.

"Is this where you sleep?" I asked. Then I realized how stupid the question was. But I couldn't help but think about him lying in that bed, hair tousled, stretched out beneath the sheets. Of course, that made me wonder how many other women have been in this bed.

"You're nervous?" He asked. "Well, don't be, my little girl. You have nothing to be nervous about. Now get under the covers and warm up for daddy."

I climbed onto his large bed, and the moment I lie back into the plush pillows, I dissolved. The feeling almost brought tears to my eyes, and I pulled the cloud-like duvet up to my nose. I questioned if I was having an out-of-body experience because these things had never happened to me. No one but Lincoln has ever cared about me. It was always him and me against the shit world. I stared up at the crystalized chandelier hanging above me and thought about the money he gave me yesterday. I checked my account almost fifty times last night to make sure it wouldn't magically disappear. Carter used his phone to dim the lights in the room before turning on soft country music. He removed his remaining clothing, which included his jeans and his boxers. Standing naked before me in his entirety, I swallowed hard and proceeded to pull the duvet past my eyes, but his fingers wrapped around the edge and tugged it back down. I tucked my knees up, covering my stomach with my arms.

"Don't you dare," he said, his tone low with a smirk on his face. "Don't do that. Let me see you. Let me look at you."

"But I'm—"

"Gorgeous? Exquisite?" He ran his fingers from my knee, up to my thigh, around my hip, and over my stomach. "Fucking delicious?"

He kissed my navel, and I giggled as his hair brushed my skin. I could feel him grinning against me. He straddled me, putting his hands on either side of my head and caging me in. Then he lowered himself, his mouth covering mine. The way he kissed me was both soft and aggressive all at the same time, and every part of me responded to it.

I pressed my hips against him, wanting to feel him. Then I reached up, running my hands over his chest, shoulders, and back. Holding himself in a push-up position had every muscle engaged, and I wanted to touch all of him.

"You're feistier than I expected," he said, pulling back just enough to look at me. "Do you want me?"

I nodded, and my cheeks warmed.

"This isn't your first time, is it?"

I shook my head. "Does that bother you?"

"The only thing that bothers me is knowing you've let others touch you. Boys that probably didn't know what the fuck they were doing. But don't worry, princess, because after I'm done with you, no one else will ever be able to make you come again."

He reached down, running the tip of his cock from my clit, where he teased me again for a moment, down to my opening. I widen my legs, bracing for it.

"Relax, sweetheart. Let daddy own you."

His words alone made me wetter. He felt it and grew even harder before pushing into me. The first thrust drowned my lungs with air, and my hands found his chest in protest. He removed them and pinned them down to the bed.

"Shh," he hushed me, kissing me softly. "Daddy's got you. Give into me. Feel me. Let it go."

Our hips began to rock, and I tightened around him. He was balls deep inside me now, and I was taken aback by how full I felt. My emotions were mixed, it all felt like too much, but at the same time, I could never get enough of him. He knew exactly how to move, and we rocked slowly for a while until I needed more.

"Daddy..." I whined.

"Yes? Tell me what you want, baby girl. Tell daddy how you want me to fuck you."

"I need..."

"Say it," he growled. "What do you want daddy to do?"

"Fuck me," I whispered.

He stopped all movement and clamped his gaze on me. "Say it again."

"Fuck me...Daddy."

If the devil had a laugh, I was certain it was Carters because it set my nerves on fire.

He pulled out just a bit and then slammed back into me before lowering his ear to my mouth. "Tell me one more time, princess. I didn't quite catch what you said."

"What are you? Hard of hearing?" The words slipped off my tongue before I could force them back down.

I braved his gaze as he studied me, and his lips parted. The fact that his hazel eyes seemed to turn a shade darker sent a wave of electricity straight to my clit.

His hand found my throat. "I am when it comes to you. Now fucking tell me what you want me to do to your little cunt."

"Make me your slut, Daddy."

He took my words with an open invitation and pounded into me over and over. His hips moved in a rhythmic motion, and he made sure to keep a thumb on my swollen clit.

"Are you going to be a good girl and come on, daddy's cock?"

The sensations sent me into a spiral so that forming a sentence wasn't even an option at the moment. The bed shook slightly, and my lids fluttered. I could only see his abs hovering above me as my breasts jiggled with the rough movements. His voice lowered an entire octave as he called me his pretty little slut on repeat. My body tensed and commanded my attention.

"Come on, my dick baby, and don't you fucking look away."

His words took control of my body, and my fingers dug into his skin. I arched my back and squeezed my legs around his torso. It hurt and felt good at the same time. Exhausted, I let my body melt into the sheets, and my posture relaxed. He lifted and pulled my legs together in the air. I peered over my thighs to catch his gaze.

"What's my favorite word, baby?" he asked as he pressed into me.

"Daddy."

His eyes rolled to the back of his head, and he pulsed inside me. Warmth drenched my folds as he filled me up. His hips jerked, and a slow grizzly moan dripped off his lips. His seed pooled out of me and circled my asshole. He gasped when he pulled out, the swollen bulb of his flesh red and angry. He took the liberty of stuffing his spilled seed back into me as it seeped out and plugged my hole with two fingers.

"You are such a fucking good girl." He gave me a kiss on the forehead and then left me as he climbed off the bed.

My inner thighs were wet, my folds sticky, and my mind in a blissful fog. He returned from the bathroom with a warm cloth and spread my legs as he wiped away his leftover mess. The sensation made me jerk, and he teased me once last time by pressing his thumb on my clit. I cried out, but he cooed at me to calm down and pressed the warm cloth into my pussy for comfort. He chucked the used cloth near the bathroom and rolled over next to me.

The lazy grin on his face disappeared when he looked into my eyes. "Brooklyn? Hey, what's the matter? Did I hurt you? Was it too much?"

His concern was genuine, and it only made the tears fall harder. I wiped them away, and he lifted his body until his back met the headboard. Pulling me into his chest, he kissed my forehead and forced my face into the nape of his neck.

"Please tell me what I did wrong?" he asked.

"You didn't do anything wrong," I choked out.

"What is it then?"

"I just... I've never been with anyone who actually cared about how I felt."

"What?" He narrowed his eyes. "No one has ever...?"

I shook my head and wiped my nose.

"Come here," he said, kissing me again. "From the first time I saw you at Estelle's, I haven't been able to stop thinking about you. I wanted you. Every inch of you."

I playfully rolled my eyes.

He winged a brow. "You think I'm lying, baby girl?"

"Look at you, Carter. You could literally have any girl you want. And I'm supposed to believe that you want me?"

"I don't like being called a liar." His voice was soft but still had a hint of teasing to it.

"And I don't like being lied to..." I said as I nudged him in the stomach.

Carter rolled me onto my back before pushing his

weight against me. Then his fingers found my belly, and I shrieked.

"Stop," I begged him, but he just grinned.

"Well, now I know your weakness."

"Daddy," I squealed. I could barely breathe.

"Not until you say it," he demanded.

"I believe you."

Finally, he stopped and lowered his lips to mine before pulling me into his embrace.

"Fuck, you felt good. Now go to sleep."

I closed my eyes and melted into the warmth of his body, and for the first time in my life, I was going to sleep without the weight of the world on my shoulders.

CHAPTER 10
Truths ~ Carter

IT TOOK everything for me to get out of bed in the morning. Brooklyn looked like an angel, lying on her stomach with her mess of fiery red hair splayed out around her pillow, with her natural curl pattern molded into her tresses. I liked it like that, wild and unkempt. I kissed her back several times, and while she didn't stir, a tiny smile played on her lips. *Fuck me.* This girl was doing more to me than I'd expected. Yes, I was attracted to her from day one. I loved how she looked so innocent all the time, like a lost little girl in need of protection. I couldn't help but eat that shit up. But I also loved the contrast. She was a woman. Every voluptuous inch of her.

I threw on a pair of jeans and dragged myself to the kitchen for a cup of liquid brain energy. My chef had a nice spread laid out an hour ago, with the hot foods laying idle on the warmer. With my coffee in hand, I sauntered to my office, taking a peek in the direction of my bedroom as I rounded the corner in the opposite direction. My home office spanned the space of my master bedroom, yet I hated working from here. Although I enjoyed the solitude, bad memories of Claire and our hellish breakup still lingered in the air. I shook the thoughts from my mind as I sank into my executive chair and moved the mouse. The sun had only been up for few hours, and already a long string of emails was waiting to be answered. I scrolled through, stopping at the one Aiden sent to me around 3 a.m. this morning. I asked him to dig into Lincoln's case, and since the information I needed wasn't available for the public eye, I knew he was the right man for the job. He owned a private security firm in Stonebridge, and he only catered his services to the elite. However, I had the pleasure of calling him an old friend, and I remembered how good of a hacker he was. The information Aiden gave me had me grinning like the Cheshire cat. Unbeknownst to both Brooklyn and Lincoln, a building across from the store had cameras, which meant they had security footage.

    I dialed Aiden's number and wired him a few extra grand for the rushed job as I waited. The rest of the morning consisted of answering emails and returning phone calls. My mind would have been in the zone on any other day, but the only thing I could think about was my bedroom and the sweet little princess lying naked, tangled in the sheets. I scanned the time on my computer and noticed the clock struck 11 a.m. a few minutes ago, yet Brooklyn was still in bed. *Damn, I wore my baby out.*

A moment later, her soft voice echoed off the walls. I realized I had never given her a tour, and I called out. She followed my voice and sauntered into my office. Her nipples pebbled through her tight-fitted cupcake dotted tank, and my eyes trailed down to her purple panties with a bow on the front. Her fuzzy-covered feet rounded my desk, and I tugged her into my lap.

"I'm hungry," she said, running her hand through her wild tresses.

I let my fingers graze over her warm, smooth skin and placed a kiss on her arm. "Lucky you, the chef made a whole spread. It's in the kitchen. Do you remember where it is?"

She twirled a lock of hair around her finger before she nodded. My phone rang, and I patted her bottom, my eyes settled on her hips as she strolled out of my office. I licked my bottom lip. It took everything in me to not pick her up and carry her back to the bedroom, but missing calls from our elite clients was something my father frowned upon, and the last thing I needed was him coming around. I took the call, nodded, and pinched the bridge of my nose the entire time. It baffled me that so many people wanted to buy but knew jack shit about real estate. Money didn't buy common sense, and damn I wished it did.

Brooklyn passed by a moment later just as I was ending the call, and I gave her a *come here* motion with my finger. She padded her way in, her eyes wide as she took in the room, a cup of coffee in hand.

"This is crazy," she said before taking a sip of her coffee.

I narrowed my eyes at her. "You were just in here."

"I know, but now I'm actually awake. I can see."

I let my tongue flick the roof of my mouth as I digested her cute fucking face.

"Mhmm. Well, I'm glad you like it."

I pulled her into my lap, and her ass landed right where I wanted it, and I wondered if she could feel just how rock-hard I was. My arms clamped around her waist, and I nipped at her neck until she turned to face me. I waited until she finished her sip and then slammed my lips onto hers.

"I haven't brushed my teeth yet." She giggled.

I kissed her again. "You're fine, princess. Did you see all the snacks in the kitchen?"

She nodded and raised her shoulders in excitement as she bopped up and down. I had to dig my teeth into her shoulder to prevent her from blowing my load due to the movement.

"It's all for you," I said, brushing her hair back. "But

daddy has to work some more. Feel free to roam around. But..." I ran my fingers down the front of her shirt, making her nipples harden. "You have to stay just like this."

"I can't get dressed?" she asked, her voice breathy from my touch.

"Is that a problem?" I lowered my tone. But the way she's batting her chocolate eyes under those long eyelashes makes forming words nearly impossible.

"No, Daddy." Those words were well-rehearsed by now and dripped from her tongue like sugar.

You have work to do, Carter.

"Run along," I told her.

I worked for a couple hours before closing my laptop for a break. The TV sound blared from the other room, and I took that as my cue to go check on her. Peeking into the living room, I found her sprawled out on the couch, with her juicy ass ripe for the taking. Her thumbs jutted across the screen as she stared at her phone. She made a few slight movements, and my eyes settled on her delectable peach, and damn did I want to take a bite out of it. A bowl of Lucky Charms sat empty on the glass table. Her head moved as she adjusted on the pillow, and I inched forward. A group of animated pets flew across the screen, and I folded my arms across my chest. So fitting for my little girl to be watching *The Secret Life of Pets* while munching on fruit and texting. She didn't notice my presence, so I let my eyes rest on her, and my heart flipped in my chest at a sudden realization. I had my pick of women, everything from models to movie stars, but nothing never stuck because all those women cared about two things. Money and appearance. But Brooklyn saw me as a human, someone more than what I could give her, and fuck, did I want to give her the world. She warmed up the frozen heart in my chest, removing the pain that settled there. I ran a hand from her ass up to her head, and she turned over before sitting up.

"Oops, sorry. I guess I should have asked before eating in the living room."

I sat down next to her. "What did I say, princess? Never apologize for anything."

"I forgot," she said meekly. "I'm just not used to it."

"Get used to it." I kissed her cheek and inhaled her sweet scent as I reached for the remote. "Tell me more about your childhood? ."

Her attention hopped between the muted tv and my gaze. A small part of me felt guilty for asking since Aiden had already filled me in, but I wanted to hear what she had to say.

"What do you want to know?"

"Everything." I stroked her hair, my fingers getting caught in the unruly curls.

"Well, I don't have parents. I never really did. Not that I remember anyway. My dad was basically a no-call-no-show in my life from day one, and my mom got sick when we were young. The only memory I have of her was picking strawberries at this farm when I was really little." Her words trailed off.

"Go on." I nudged my nose against her cheek.

"I remember them tasting like sunshine and pure sugar. I guess it's why I like sweets so much." She smiled at the memory and then placed her head on my chest.

A rage of fire boiled my blood as I thought about her father. Fucking deadbeat. Leaving my princess and her brother to fend for themselves.

Her smile faded a little. "It's probably why I'm so…"

"Lovely?" I interrupted.

"Is that really what guys want, though?" she asked, looking at me.

"It's what *men* want," I emphasized.

She opened her mouth a little as if to say something but stopped. I tipped my chin, urging her to go on.

"Why aren't you married?"

I was willing to talk to her about anything. But I had to admit, that one threw me for a curve.

"It's just that you're rich. You're attractive, and you're not…young." She was careful about the last word.

"I was engaged once." I drew in a breath and wished I had a drink in my hand.

Her eyes focused on my expression, and I spilled the beans of my last serious relationship. Her hands covered her mouth in shock as I hashed out the fucked-up details, and once I got it all out, she placed a kiss on my lips.

"That's terrible, Carter." She swung her arms around my neck and gave me another intoxicating kiss.

Even in the seriousness of this moment, I liked the way my name sounded rolling off her tongue.

I sighed. "It's probably for the best."

"How can you say that, though?" she asked, almost defensively.

"Because I found you," I said before stealing a kiss.

A familiar but buried feeling flooded over me in hot waves. I wanted to take her to my bedroom. I wanted to fuck her. To make her mine, over and over again. But not for a baby. Not for any motive outside of my heart choosing her, and there was nothing I could do to change that.

Suddenly her phone rang, jolting us both from the kiss. "Who is it?" I asked, unable to mask my annoyance.

She stood. "It's the jail. It might be Lincoln."

I nodded, and she answered.

CHAPTER 11
Confessions ~ Brooklyn

I STEPPED AWAY from the couch and headed down the hall. I needed some privacy.

"Lincoln?"

"How in the hell did you do it?" he blurted into the phone.

I stopped. "Do what, Lincoln? I didn't do anything. Just hang on. Give me a few minutes, and we will be right there."

"You're telling me you had nothing to do with the lawyer that showed up to represent me? He's the real deal! Like...the prosecutor almost shit himself when he saw this dude walk in." He stopped for a moment, his tone changing. "Wait, we? Whose we?"

I shook my head, the words catching in my throat, and I felt Carter's hand on my shoulder. I looked up at him, and he took the phone from me, ending the call.

"What did you do?" The words tumbled out of my mouth.

He took a step forward and placed his hands on my waist. "I think it's best if you let me handle things from now on," he said.

"I asked what you did." My pulse quickened as I waited for his response.

I expected him to be upset and tell me not to talk back. But instead, Carter handed me my phone and led me to the bedroom. He motioned for me to sit on the bed, and he walked over to the window.

"I have a friend. He's an investigator, and considering your brother's predicament, I felt I needed more information about the situation.

I shook my head a little. "But Carter. I didn't ask you to help. I just needed the money. That's why I'm here, right? You're paying me for a child, and in turn, I was going to get my brother a lawyer that actually gave him a fair chance at proving his innocence."

"I know, it's just..." He struggled for the words before coming over to the bed.

He kneeled in front of me and took my hands in his. "I have access to the best the world has to offer, baby girl. I can get anything you could ever want or need for you, and this lawyer will see to it that your brother never sees a courtroom. The next time you talk to him, it won't be on jail visitation. He's going to walk free, Brooklyn. Today."

I just stared at him. It didn't seem possible. "But... why? Why would you do all this for me before I even give you what you want?" My stomach pitted in tight coils as I digested the whole situation.

"Because you are what I want."

His words stunted my tongue, and my heartbeat halted in my chest. I pulled back instinctively.

"I don't understand. I thought this was a business transaction. I am contracted to you."

"And I am indebted to you." His voice shook with vulnerability, and his forehead found mine. "Before I met you, I was a shell of a man. But the day I met you, I felt alive. You did something to me, little girl. You made me feel things I never have before, and now that I've felt that, I don't know if I can live without it. Without you."

His words nearly shattered me, and I wanted to believe them. Truly, I did. But it wasn't that simple for me. It never had been. "You hardly know me," I said softly. "How can you be so sure?"

Carter stood as he pulled my hand toward his chest. "Do you feel that? The way my heart is racing? No one has ever made it do that. That's how daddy knows, baby girl."

I swallowed and met his gaze. This entire time I thought everything I was feeling was a fluke. The way he made butterflies swarm in my stomach when he smiled, the way he made me scream out his name as he brought me to ecstasy, and the way he made me feel like the only girl in the world. I've only known this man for seventy-two hours, but if someone asked me if I wanted to spend the rest of my life with him, I would say yes in a heartbeat. As if he could read my thoughts, he let my hand go and turned in the direction of his walk-in closet.

"We need to get dressed to go see your brother."

"You're coming with me?" I stood in a swift motion and placed my hand on my chest.

He stepped out of his closet and pulled a soft polo shirt over his head. "Of course. Anything that concerns you concerns me."

"Oh, okay. I mean, I know you're busy, and you've already done—"

Before finishing my sentence, he closed the space between us, and his mouth crashed onto mine. He nearly brought me to my knees. His kisses were breathtaking but not forceful. Gearing up to break away, he pulled me closer, deepening our kiss until every nerve in my body went up in flames. It was so soft it nearly brought me to my knees. When the kiss finally ended, the room was spinning, and I lowered my feet back down to the carpet.

"I told you, little girl. Daddy is going to take care of everything."

I threw on a pair of jeans and a t-shirt. Once I had

all my things together, he grabbed my hand and pulled me toward the door.

CHAPTER 12
New Beginnings ~ Carter

THE CAR WAS WAITING for us when we got downstairs, and it killed me to let go of her hand to open the passenger side door. She climbed in and then I followed suit. I hated myself for not telling her my true feelings from the beginning, the beginning being three days ago, but she was my end. Being with her made me realize it wasn't about the baby or appeasing my father. It was about her and me and the possibility of us. My father taught me that actions always spoke louder than words, and what better way to express my love toward her than lifting the heaviest boulder off her shoulders.

Stroking her thigh, I opened my mouth to speak when my phone vibrated in my pocket. I pulled it out, took a peek, and ignored the call. My father, of course. He never beat around the bush, and he only called for two reasons. Important business and our lawyer. Our family lawyer was the best of the best, but my father paid him, and he had a hard time keeping secrets from the old bastard. I ignored the second set of vibrations and returned my attention to my baby girl. As I took her in, I found myself comparing the contrast in our styles. I changed into a pair of slacks and a dark colored polo, and here she was wearing faded denim jeans and a unicorn-themed t-shirt with high-top tennis shoes. I loved it, though. I loved her.

"Hey," I said softly, putting my hand on her thigh. "You look nervous."

"I am," she said as a frosty look etched its way onto her features.

"You have nothing to be nervous about, princess. I told you, daddy took care of everything."

"It's not just that..." she trailed off. "It's me. It's Lincoln. Our life. We don't live in the same world as you do. You're rich and respected and—"

I cut her off right there because I didn't want to hear it. I picked her up by her waist and lifted her to my lap. She resisted, but I just pulled her into me and pressed my face into the softness of her curls.

"I told you, you are what I want."

"Even if I'm a trainwreck?" she asked, taking in a sharp breath.

I tightened my grip around her soft waist and separated her legs with my knee. "Yes."

"And my life is a dumpster fire?"

"A gorgeous dumpster fire," I said, grazing the shell of her ear.

"And my brother is a walking disaster?"

"My younger brother is in the looney bin. How's that for disaster?"

"Seriously?" Her interest piqued, and she turned in my lap.

I nodded in a slow and sinister manner. My movements made her giggle, and I forgot how much I loved to hear her laugh.

"Well, shit. Yeah, that's pretty bad," she teased me, and I loved it.

I spun her around until she was straddling me, and her breasts were inches from my face.

"Listen. How about we make a new deal, hmm? How about I make you mine forever, and you'll never have to worry about anything else in your life. Pain-in-the-ass-brother included in the deal."

She studied me. "Is that really want you want?"

I cupped her face in my palms. "Baby girl, that's *all* daddy wants."

As much as I hated how my father dictated my life, I couldn't help but be a little grateful that he rode my ass so hard. If he hadn't, I wouldn't have never met Brooklyn.

Once we arrived at the jail, I took her hand and led her inside. Security check was a breeze, and I took her hand once more and brought it to my lips, kissing it reassuringly. A buzzer sounded, and a steel door glided open. The lawyer stood once he caught sight of me, and Brooklyn tore her hand from mine as she ran up to her brother. The loss of her touch was abrupt, but I let her go, my heart swelling in my chest as they embraced.

CHAPTER 13
She's a real Good Girl~Carter

Six Months Later

"CAN WE JUST LIVE HERE?" Brooklyn mumbled from the other room. We were in the Maldives for a little impromptu pre-honeymoon. Six months had passed since I asked her to stay with me forever. I proposed to her a week after she officially moved into my house.

"Is our penthouse no longer up to par?" I asked, stepping into the bedroom.

"It's all right, I guess." She enjoyed getting under my skin and being a little brat.

"And this vacation suite? Does it meet the future Mrs. Castle's standards?"

"It'll do." The words dripped from her lips nonchalantly.

I peered in her direction as I poured myself a drink. Her luscious pregnant body was sprawled out on the bed, and her eyes locked on the blood-orange sky. She complained about the shape of belly because it was in the shape of a B and often tried to hide it from me, but I was stubborn. No matter how many dips it formed I wanted her naked at all times with her belly on display for me to touch, kiss and admire. I stared at her, and I knew she could feel it because her mouth twitched in a smirk. *God, she was perfect.* Like unreal. We've been here for a couple days, and it's been bliss. Once she accepted my invitation to move in, I let her re-decorate to her liking. Positive that I would come home one day to pink walls and a bedroom full of stuffed animals, she shocked me with her good taste. Soft couches, accent pieces, and flavorful candles littered our home, and it was perfect.

I let my father know that I was done letting him push me around. Giving him an heir to Castle Realty was less of a priority than loving my fiancée. I made sure he understood that when the twins were born, they wouldn't be part of the family business. They would grow up like every other kid, eat junk, go to summer camp, and get dirty. A "luxury" I never had.

"What are you thinking about, Daddy?" she asked as she struggled to roll over on her back.

I swallowed my sip. "You. Did you call your brother?"

I hooked Lincoln up with a studio apartment, but he had to agree to get his GED. Turned out the kid was pretty damn smart. He enrolled at Stonebridge Technical college and majored in mechanical studies. I asked Aiden if he knew anyone who could give the kid a chance with his record and wouldn't ask questions. Lucky for Lincoln, Aiden had a friend who owned a towing company. His name was Dylan.

"Yeah. He has tons of homework, so he didn't talk long."

"Mmhmm."

She turned to face me and then rolled her head back to the other side. She was so fucking cute. I rounded the front of the bed, forcing my length into her line of sight. She used to look away. Now she just licked her lips and teased me.

"I gave you all this. A good girl would tell daddy thank you…"

"And if I don't?" she purred.

I bit my lip and grabbed the sheet to yank it off her. "Then daddy might have to rip it all away."

She shrieked, her body curling up defensively, and I pounced on the bed. I straddled her, putting my hands on either side of her head to cage her in as I leaned down, devouring her neck.

"You smell like candy."

"I taste like it too…"

I pulled away enough to look at her. She gave me a

small "innocent" smile, and I kissed down between her breasts, down over her Pooh Bear belly, taking my time around her navel because it made her giggle, and I fucking *loved* how girly and cute that sound was before my mouth closed around her sweet cunt. Fuck, it was sweet. Very sweet.

"What is that?" I asked, focusing on the round candy between her lips.

"Cherry cordials," she said, holding her hand open. "Compliments of the hotel. You want one?"

I bit the candy out of her hand. It had a chocolate shell with syrup on the inside and, of course, a maraschino cherry. The juices spilled down my chin and onto her hard nipples when I bit into it.

I grinned wickedly before licking it off. My touch made her back arch and her lips part. Soft whimpers left her lips, and my hand found her sensitive clit. I worked it and refused to break my eye contact. I now knew exactly how to make her wither, and it didn't take long for her to reach the edge. She had sensitive nipples that begged to be sucked and a clit that responded if stroked in a rapid movement. Her hands found their way into my hair as she gasped for air. Her body froze, and that little cry that made my cock a dripping mess oozed off her tongue. I took until she forced my mouth from her pussy. I resisted because I loved making her cry in pleasure and witnessing her become a mess under my touch. I lifted and focused on the jerking movements her body made from my tongue.

"Oh, we aren't done, sweetheart. Not even close."

"But you already filled me up this morning and afternoon. I can't take anymore." She pouted her lips in protest.

I stroked her soft cheeks, wiping away the leftover tears of pleasure I made her shed. Her hair was in two pigtail buns, and her soft feet were covered with a pair of fluffy pink socks.

"I want you leaking my seed, baby girl. Did you bring some tampons with you?"

She tilted her head. "Yes, but I'm not on mother nature at the moment."

I got up and headed to the bathroom. Taking a peek inside her cream-colored makeup bag, I picked up a yellow-covered wrapped tampon.

Returning to my original position, I spread her legs, exposing her sweet cunt, and ran the tip of my angry cock along her slit. I teased her before shoving it inside, and the gasp that she let out nearly killed me. My thumb found her clit as I sat inside her, and she shoved my hand away. I returned it, and her eyes closed. I found so much joy in witnessing her whine. It was almost addictive. My thumb tortured her, and tears plucked at the corner of her eyes. Shoving my thumb into her mouth, she sucked, and I pulled out before ramming back into her. I could never hold on for long with her. Her tightness was a blessing and a curse. In one final thrust, I erupted, and hot liquid flowed through her.

My cock pulsed against her walls. "That's my girl. Take daddy's cum. You're such a good fucking girl."

I grabbed the tampon and ripped the wrapping from it. Her eyes widened, and I pulled out, my flesh dripping. I shoved the blue plastic tampon inside and extracted the plastic casing before leaning back to admire my work. She lifted her head, unsuccessfully peering over her large belly.

"You plugged me?" A hint of shock coated her words.

Leaning over, I caught her bottom lip between my teeth. "Fuck yeah. Are you daddy's little cum dumpster?"

She nodded and nestled her head back into the soft pillow.

"Good girl."

Daddy's Filthy Obsession

CHAPTER 1
The Fidelity Test ~Cora

"JOSH, you know I want to wait before we go to second base," I said as I ran my fingers through his sandy blond hair.

He sucked in his cheeks and let out a disappointed puff of air as he let his head fall into the nape of my neck. "C'mon, babe. You're killing me. Let me smash that tight little kitty."

"Shh! You can't talk to me like that when my dad is home. He could come up here and hear you." I tugged at the collar of his t-shirt, and he pulled his bottom lip between his teeth.

"Your first time will be special, Cora. I have a blanket in the back of my car. It's new. Never been used."

"How exhilarating. Getting laid in the back of your shit car." I dropped my eyes to my phone and giggled when I saw a text from my best friend slide across the screen.

Josh lowered his lips to the nape of my neck. His wet tongue poked me in an attempt to try and turn me on. I shifted, elbowing him in the gut to get him to stop.

"Fuck. How long are you going to make me wait? All my friends are getting laid. I'm tired of—"

"Tired of what?" My dad poked his head through the door, and I shoved Josh off of me. Sitting up, I ran my hands through my hair and climbed off the bed.

"Nothing. Josh is just talking about school stuff." I held my breath and released it when dad relayed a soft smile. "What's up? Did you burn the brats for the party and need me to run to the store?"

He jutted his tongue into his cheek and scratched the edge of his grin. "I can't find my other pair of jeans. I thought I—"

"Bottom drawer of your dresser." I climbed off the bed and grabbed his wrist as I pulled him out of my room and into his.

"What would I do without you, sweet pea?"

I rolled my eyes and shook my head. He was right, though. He would perish without me, although he tried to tell himself every day that he had everything under control. He had nothing under control. He would be wearing a two-week-old shirt and grease-stained jeans if I didn't wash his clothing like clockwork. A clean house with a fridge full of food and bills that were paid on time was all my doing. Sometimes I wondered if he let me take the reins because he was afraid to.

"Here. I put them at the bottom because you rarely wear your nice ones." He placed a soft kiss on my cheek and took the jeans from my hands.

A beat of silence passed between us, and I waited patiently for the thoughts running through his head to spill off his lips, but before he could, my gaze locked on the bedroom door.

"Am I interrupting?" My dad's girlfriend sauntered in. Her four-inch wedge sandals glided across the carpet as she nestled behind my dad. She peered over his shoulder and locked her icy blue eyes with mine.

"Nope. Just helping my dad find his clothing for the millionth time."

"Oh, God. You make it sound like a chore," he joked.

An annoying giggle flowed off her lips, and I wished I didn't have to hear it. Her name was Jewel, and she was a life-sized barbie who lived for kale salads, high heels, and expensive eye cream. Not much younger than my dad, she cast off her sons years ago and set on a journey to find true love; sadly, she ended up here. She ran her manicured fingers through her platinum tresses before she snatched my dad's lips. The image made me wince, and I walked around them and headed for the hallway.

"Did you tell her?" she whispered in my dad's ear.

I turned reluctantly and shoved my hands into the back pockets of my shorts. "Tell me what?"

My heart dropped into my stomach as I waited. I had a hunch what they were going to say, and the thought turned my stomach sour. My dad stepped toward me and grabbed my hand. He was obviously just as nervous because it looked like he was going to vomit.

"I know," I blurted out before his lips parted.

His brows furrowed, and he sliced his gaze back to Jewel before returning them to me. "You know…?"

I folded my arms across my chest and jutted my hip. "Hiding rings in socks isn't such a good idea, Dad."

"Are you upset, sweet pea?" He dipped his chin and trailed a thumb over his lip.

I traded a glance between him and Jewel before begrudgingly opening my arms and plastering a smile across my face. My dad's eyes lit up, and he pulled me into his embrace.

"I hid the ring in a sock?" he asked, his brows furrowing as he rehashed his actions.

"Yeah. It fell out of one when I was reorganizing your sock drawer." I blew out my cheeks, gearing up to break the beat of awkward silence when the doorbell saved me.

Jewel clapped her hands like a five year and hurried to the door. "The cake is here." Her blonde hair trailed behind her, and I bit the inside of my cheeks as I watched her leave the room.

Before I could even ask dad about his future marriage plans, her annoying voice stole his attention, letting him know the one guy he hated the most had arrived.

"You invited Brett? Why?"

I closed the gap between us and placed my hands on my hips. I didn't want to believe it. My dad and Brett were childhood friends and stopped talking years ago. My dad swore that he would never again give him the time of day after their falling out.

He walked over to the bedroom door, closing it until only a sliver of the hallway was visible. "I needed to make sure. After your mom left me—"

"Mom left you because you gave up on her. You gave up on us. So, what is it that you have to make sure of?" I said, interrupting him.

He licked his lips, and a flush crept across his cheeks. He was never good at telling a lie, and I had a knack for knowing when he was pulling my leg.

"I need to make sure I can trust her. I have to be sure she's really here for me...and you."

"Are you serious right now? A fucking fidelity test

with your ex-best friend who you hate and is five years younger than you?"

"Language sweet pea," he scolded.

He raised his chin to the ceiling and swallowed. I guess he was trying to find the words that made this whole thing make sense, but there were no words. I dropped my arms to my side and pulled open the door. Sadness crept into his features, and I turned to head down the stairs.

My dad had decided to invite a few guys from his tow company over for a cookout. Josh's voice carried from the backyard. He wasted no time shoving fresh off the grill brats in his mouth as he hung off Jewel like a lazy sloth. My name dripped off the tongues of the guests in greeting as I stepped through the sliding door, and Brett's eyes locked on mine. I broke our gaze and headed straight to the pool. The August air strangled me with each breath I took, and if I didn't get into something cool asap, I would probably pass out.

"Can I join you?" Jewel yelled from the grill.

She didn't wait for an answer. *So typical.* Peeling off what little clothing she had on, she jumped into the pool, splashing me with the icy water. I swam to the other side and found solace in the tiny patch of shade away from Brett's piercing stare, which he refused to break.

CHAPTER 2
The Encounter ~ Brett

HIS HOUSE still looked the same, and he still had that old beat-up muscle car. I remembered the day he bought it. He loved it and refused to give it up, even when he knew his girlfriend at the time was pregnant with Cora. To say I was shocked when I saw a missed call from Dylan Lane slide across my screen was an understatement. I hadn't spoken to him in over four years. Our friendship ended when I decided to book a one-way ticket to California without him.

I waited, gearing up my resolve in case he'd just wanted to bring me all this way to punch me in the face, although I deserved it. The door opened, and my eyes lingered on the pair of long tanned legs before I met the gaze of a woman with blonde hair and fake breasts. She motioned me inside with a wide smile, and I followed her to the backyard. His house had been updated, new furniture and a few pieces of art I knew he didn't buy. The blonde woman made it a point to be the center of attention, but Cora pulled me in once I stepped through the sliding door. Hair darker than midnight, with curves that would shame a special edition Mustang GT. Cora was no longer a little girl, and the two-piece swimsuit she sported was the proof in the pudding. She was juicy in all the right places, and damn did my cock take notice. I downed my drink and begged for my flesh to back down.

No matter how severed Dylan's and my friendship was, the bro code was still intact, and I could never. *Well, they do say never say never.* Unable to pry my eyes away, a wave of relief washed over me when she turned her back to my gaze. Now she wouldn't know that I just spent ten minutes staring at her delectable bubble butt as she stood in the shallow water. I turned to chit-chat with a few of the guys. Some I remembered back from technical college, which made the awkwardness that loomed in the air more tolerable. Dylan gave me a nod, and I returned the favor. Whatever harsh words he had for me, he planned on waiting until his guests were gone before giving me an earful.

Refocusing on the greasy burger in front of me, everyone's attention was stolen when the blonde woman yelped from the pool playfully. Her colorful bikini top was no longer wrapped around her overly tanned neck and was now floating away from her. All the guys had a good laugh, but the only swim top I was worried about was Cora's. Dylan announced unexpectedly that he had to leave because one of the tow trucks got into an accident. A wave of low grumbles and mumbles trickled off the lips of his guests. The blonde's whiny voice begged him to stay, but it did nothing to persuade him. Placing his plate down and shoving his phone into his pocket, he headed inside the house, and most of the guys followed.

The blonde apologized to the thinning crowd, which consisted of me, Cora, and some guy I didn't know. *Now, this is awkward.* Reaching for the metal bars, the blonde pulled herself from the pool without even bothering to cover up. I downed my drink and made myself stupidly useful at the grill as I flipped an already badly burned burger. Refusing to make eye contact, she grabbed her phone off a nearby table and went inside. The guy who'd lingered near Cora locked his eyes on the blonde and followed soon after.

My blood warmed, and I didn't know if it was from the soul-sucking sun or the fact that Cora's nipples pebbled through her floral bathing suit.

"Last time I saw you, you were begging for a ride to go see some chick flick." I eased in, closing in on the wide gap between us.

She walked over, tossing her long tresses over one shoulder before wringing them out. The leftover water dripped onto her bathing suit, amplifying her swollen nipples, and my dick throbbed.

"You have a bad memory. What, do you have Alzheimer's or something?"

"Ouch. You're not in school for nursing, are you?" I gave her a sheepish smile as I sipped on my drink.

"FYI, it was a thriller." She tilted her head to the side and pushed some chips past her kissable lips. "Do you know why you're here?"

I swallowed and set my cup on the edge of the table. "I was hoping you could fill me in."

She folded her arms across her chest, propping up her pillow-soft breasts. "Dad wanted to see if you were still a douche bag."

I pursed my lips and nodded. "Well, I haven't been that guy in a long time. Playboy Brett died years ago."

"Whatever. I can't tell you if you passed his little test." She shrugged and lifted the plastic cup to her lips.

With questions on the edge of my tongue, she turned and stormed off into the house. Chalking it up to teenage emotions, I sauntered over to a comfortable lawn chair nestled under the large tree. Unfortunately, my attempt at getting comfortable and finishing off this bottle of beer was interrupted when a scream erupted from upstairs.

CHAPTER 3
Salacious Truths ~ Cora

EVERY MUSCLE in my body tensed as I looked at the sights happening before me. It was as if I had been thrown into an alternate universe, with my worst nightmare coming to life. My longtime boyfriend, the guy who I planned my whole life around, the guy I was going to marry and eventually lose my virginity to, was straddled on top of Jewel, with his cock nestled comfortably between her fake tits. They stumbled off of my bed, and I never wanted to burn something so badly in my life. Jewel scrambled to a corner, with her arms crossed across her chest, and Josh fell to his knees in front of me.

Groveling soon commenced, his lips moved, and with furrowed brows his hands found my wrist. I heard nothing, muteness surrounded me, and my eyes burned.

"Babe, please..." Josh held on to my wrist, the nails of his fingers digging into my flesh.

I pulled away, my sight now a blurry mess due to the tears pooling up on the edge of my lashes.

I took a step back and then another until my back met a hard chest. I turned to find Brett wide-eyed as he sliced his gaze from Josh then to Jewel before his eyes settled on me.

"Babe," Josh pleaded from his knees.

His hand landed on my ankle, and it made my stomach churn. Brushing past Brett, I ran down the stairs and grabbed my keys off the hook near the front door. My brain was in a fog, and my emotions were a mess. My legs sprinting toward my car. Ignoring Brett's voice, I pulled out of the driveway.

My throat thick with sobs—Adele blasting from the speakers. I didn't hear the pop of my tire, and my heart dropped into my stomach as I swerved into oncoming traffic. Angry honks accompanied by a string of curse words seeped off the tongues of irritated drivers, and I pulled to the side of the road and slammed on the brakes. I thought this day couldn't get any worse, and then a fire engine red pickup truck slowed behind me, and Brett hopped down from the driver's side. Wiping the tears from my eyes, I pushed open my door and climbed out.

"I don't need your help," I spat as I kicked my sandal at the busted tire.

"I find that hard to believe."

He sauntered closer, his boots crushing dirt and rocks with each step. I dropped my chin to my chest. Here I was, on the side of the road, in a swimsuit, with damp hair and a busted tire. Steel toed boots came into my line of sight and a calloused finger clipped under my chin.

"You okay?" His voice was soft and his gaze softer.

I snapped my chin away. "Do I look like I'm okay? This is all your fault." I shoved my fingers into his chest, hoping to push him away, but he stayed planted.

"Is it?"

"Yeah, it is," I deadpanned. I lifted and placed my hands on my hips. "If you hadn't come, then none of this would have happened." I placed my palms to my cheeks, covering my embarrassment.

He stepped closer, the strong scent of sweat and cologne filling my lungs with each ragged breath. "Are you going to fill me in, or do I have to guess?" The corner of his mouth lifted to one side, and I hated myself for wanting to keep my eyes on his.

I told him he was only invited to the party because dad was doing a fidelity test, but once the words slipped off my tongue, waves of tears trickled down my cheeks, because the joke was obviously on me. I turned my back to him and leaned against my car.

My skin burned from the scorching metal, but I'd

rather feel that than the pain that tightened around my heart. Hoping he would take that as his cue to leave, he did the opposite and closed the space between us; the fabric of his shirt pressing into my back sent tingles down my spine.

"Maybe you need to see the glass half full instead of half-empty, baby girl."

He turned me to face him, his calloused thumb found my cheek, and he swiped away the fallen tears. I should have been pulling away, widening the gap between us, but instead, my body sizzled to his touch, like it was secretly trying to tell me something. My mind was a mess...and so was my heart. A tornado of rage and dejection ripped me to shreds. Maybe that's why yielded to his soft chocolate eyes. If I thought this day couldn't get any worse, I was wrong, because he leaned in, and instead of pushing him away, I tugged at his shirt and my parted lips met his. Brett's tongue dove in and danced with mine, and then he pulled away. Not thinking, I chased his lips, finding only air. I opened my eyes to find him turning back toward his truck.

He grabbed a tire iron and got to work getting my spare tire out of my trunk.

"This donut is only a temporary fix, you're going to need a new tire. I'll pick one up."

"It's fine. Dad has a few spare tires in the garage. One of those should be a match.

He wiped his hands on his already dirty jeans.

He stepped closer to me and tucked a piece of hair behind my ear. "Ever drove on a donut?"

I shook my head and ran my hand up and down my arm.

"Don't go over 50 mph and try to avoid potholes. See ya back at the house?" He waited for my answer, so I begrudgingly nodded. That was the last place I wanted to go back to. I climbed into the driver's seat and started the car. Making a U-turn in the middle of the road, he copied my actions and stayed on my ass the entire way home.

CHAPTER 4
Forbidden Fruit ~ Brett

FUCK ME. I went in for a hug and ended up with my tongue in her mouth. Goddamn, it felt good. She felt good. This was wrong, so wrong. I couldn't have her, and I shouldn't want her, but it's like she woke something in me. Like she unlocked my deepest primal instincts, and the only thing I wanted to do was mount her to my bed and spread her legs apart as I fucked every bad memory out of her juicy body. She chased after my lips, and it felt like a punch to the gut walking away from her, but I had to. My cock ached for a little girl old enough to be my daughter. *Fuck me.*

CHAPTER 5
Summer Plans ~ Cora

THE NEXT DAY...

"HOW LONG ARE you going to be gone?"

I ignored Emma's question as I continued to stuff my clothing and other things into my duffle bag. I paused for a second, counting under my breath the number of days I'd be gone versus the number of shorts I had already packed. When I got back to the house yesterday my dad was still out. I told Brett that he probably wouldn't be back until late. Not wanting to spend a minute longer in my own home, I texted Emma and told her to come pick me up. I walked over to my dresser and yanked it open, it didn't budge, and I forgot that this was the one drawer that always stuck. I pulled again and the knob came loose.

"See, this is a sign. You can't get in your drawer, which means you can't leave," Emma said as she got comfortable on my bed.

I kicked the bottom drawer and it fell open, exposing a stack of tank tops and denim shorts. "Looks like the clothing Gods are on my side," I said as I snatched up the pile and walked back over to the bed.

Emma peeked inside the duffle, and she pouted. "If it's just going to be you at the cabin, why do you need so many clothes?" Her words came out muffled due to the handful of small cookies she'd shoved into her mouth a few seconds ago.

I rolled my eyes and sighed. The light from the sun cascaded into my room, landing in the corner where the ball of wrinkled bed sheets lay. If I could burn the whole damn room, I would have. I refused to sleep here last night and spent the night at Emma's. A tightness formed in my chest as I rehashed the events that took place yesterday, but it wasn't the cheating that particularly made me sad; it was the fact that I'd ignored all the signs. I looked around the room once more and made sure I didn't forget anything.

"You know there are no laundromats near me, right?" I said as I placed my hands on my hips.

"Right..." She raised a brow and blew out her cheeks. "So you're just going to leave me? What am I supposed to do all summer?"

I snatched a cookie out of the container she held and tossed my heavy duffel to the floor. "Aren't you leaving for Europe in like a week?"

"But that's a week away. So you're making me fend for myself until I leave." She stomped her foot on the soft carpet.

Emma liked to pretend she couldn't live without me, but that was far from the truth. In reality, it was the other way around. Although Emma and I were two peas in a pod, we didn't look it. She was supermodel thin, with legs for days and a pout that would make any boy who has gone through puberty drop to his knees.

Both of her parents were cosmetic surgeons, and they spent the school year here in the suburbs and their summers galavanting around Europe. Emma was like honey to a bee, and all she had to do to catch a hot guy was to exist. I, on the other hand, had a much harder time. I had no desire to be thin. I liked the way I looked even if it meant that my favorite brand of jeans couldn't handle my thunder thighs and large ass.

"You'll be fine. Isn't there like a long line of guys waiting outside your bedroom window?" I teased and tossed the stuffed animal sitting on my bed at her head. That was the only thing I envied about Emma. She'd cashed in her V card the summer before we started college, and I'd been carrying mine around in the hopes that Josh would make it a night that I would never forget.

"This is stupid. It's not like you're going to see Josh or something. I mean, after yesterday, I heard he skipped town for the summer, so why do you have to leave?"

Her spine stiffened, and she lowered her eyes. The corners of my eyes burned, and I blinked to try and relive the uncomfortable feeling. I didn't care if Josh skipped town. I didn't care if he got hit by a damn bus at this point. I needed to be alone, away from everyone and everything.

"He just posted a picture of you on his—"

"Cora, come down here," my dad called me from the kitchen, cutting off Emma mid-sentence.

One thing about my dad, he was a mastermind at hiding his true feelings. You could tell him the world was ending, and he would shrug it off as he sipped his cup of coffee. I didn't tell him what happened between Josh and Jewel. I'd left that bag of trash for Jewel to air out all by herself. I couldn't tell if my dad had been shocked by the news or not, but the sadness in his eyes was evident. It appeared he'd taken Jewel's actions at face value and called off their relationship. When I came in this morning I saw a highball glass sitting on the kitchen island with a sip of brown liquor resting at the bottom. Dad only drank hard liquor when shit hit the roof, and I couldn't imagine the ache he felt when Jewel's cheating came to light last night. It hurt seeing the evidence, my dad popped the top on the bottle of scotch he hadn't touched in over six years.

I packed the last of my things into my backpack and swung it over my shoulders. Emma grabbed my duffle, and I raised a brow as she picked it up with ease.

"I thought you were just a Barbie girl?" I joked.

She turned, raising her arm as she showed off her muscle. "I'm Buff Barbie."

We headed down the steps. Emma dropped my duffle on the kitchen floor and grabbed some fruit off the tray sitting on the center island. Sporting a t-shirt with the sleeves rolled halfway up his arm and dishcloth hanging over his shoulder, dad turned to face me.

"Dad…" I said as I let my words trail off.

It became hard to breathe, the air thick, almost suffocating with each breath. Puffed crescent moons laid under his eyes as his wild tresses sat atop his head. A cloud of disappointment and sadness hollowed him out, and it was the most painful thing to watch.

He folded his arms across his chest and leaned his back against the edge of the sink. "Eat."

"I'll get food on the way. It's already after 11 AM. I need to leave now or—"

"Eat," he said, cutting me off. He took another sip of his coffee as he eyed my movements.

I plopped down into the chair and slid the warm plate over. A small stack of pancakes and slices of thick bacon greeted me. Refusing to break his eye contact with me, I gave in, and Emma did the honors of pouring a stream of golden syrup on top of the pancakes.

"So helpful. Thanks."

She smiled and snatched a piece of bacon off my plate before pushing it past her lips. I devoured my food, taking big bites so I could finish and get on the road.

"I need the keys, Dad."

"The keys for?" Dad teases.

My shoulders slumped, and I pierced my fork into a fluffy pancake as I bit the inside of my cheek. Sounds of him rummaging through one of the drawers stole my attention, and he dangled a pair of keys attached to a blue lanyard in front of me. I extended my hands, ready to catch them.

"I'll call once I'm there. Promise."

He walked behind me, and I tilted my head to the ceiling so he could place a quick kiss on my forehead. "Better. Drive safe and no texting and driving."

With my rebuttal on my tongue, the chime of the doorbell stole dad's attention. He walked out of the kitchen, and Emma held her phone up to my face.

"What?" I asked as I rolled my eyes.

"Check your email." An evil grin spread across her face, and I slapped her phone out of her hand. No surprise, Emma had signed me up for one of those hookup dating sites. All those guys wanted one thing, and I'd made a promise to myself that I wouldn't lose my virginity in the bathroom of a bar.

"No. Delete it."

Emma raised her chin to the ceiling and let out a long, drawn-out moan. "Oh, come on! You'll get plenty of matches. Finding someone new to fawn over will have you forgetting all about—"

"Shh!" I spat as I shoved her phone out of my line of sight.

My posture stiffened when my dad re-entered the kitchen. I was certain that Josh had skipped town because of my dad. If he saw Josh, he would kill him. Another pair of boots scraped against the wooden floor, and my gaze locked onto Brett's. If I thought the air couldn't get any thicker, I was wrong, and a fog so dense had my mouth wide, and my thoughts scrambled.

CHAPTER 6
Primal Instincts ~ Brett

YESTERDAY WAS the biggest shit show I had ever seen. After making sure Cora got home, I switched out the donut for a real tire and got the hell out of there before Dylan came back to find his life blown up. I didn't get a wink of sleep last night because my brain had refused to shut down. It had refused to stop thinking about Cora and her soft lips. I wanted so much more of her. I begrudgingly crawled out of the hotel bed this morning in an attempt to get my shit together so I could talk to Dylan.

I had planned to talk to him at the cookout, but obviously, those plans went to shit. I wasn't mad at the fact that he used me as some sort of pussy hungry bachelor to conduct his fidelity test. I used to live that life, a life with a different woman in my bed every weekend. I enjoyed the rush of having a new set of warm lips wrapped around my cock when I woke in the morning. The old me would have lived up to Dylan's expectations, flirting with Jewell to test her loyalty, but not anymore. Whoever said life couldn't knock you on your ass and force your hand was wrong because that's exactly what happened to me.

I texted Dylan a few hours after I woke up and told him I was coming over. He replied with "OK." The drive from the hotel back to his house had my pulse slamming into my neck. A part of me was dreading dealing with the elephant in the room and another part of me was fixated on the secret kiss I had with Cora. With heavy footsteps and a tight stomach, I'd followed him into the kitchen, and then my mouth watered. The lingering smell of bacon and homemade pancakes in the air had zero to do with my salivating, but the young girl with raven-colored locks and big doe eyes did. *Cora.*

"Forgetting all about who?" Dylan asked as he caught Cora's gaze.

Cora picked at her fingernails as she bit down on her juicy bottom lip. "Shirts. Matching shirts," she blurted out.

I lowered my chin and walked over to the center island, wrangling with my emotions as I tried to bite back a smile. Dylan had always been terrible when it came to spotting a lie, especially one from his daughter.

"Right," he said as he took a sip from his coffee mug.

"About Josh?" I asked as I shoved my hands into my front pockets. The room went still...as if I'd ripped a band-aide off a fresh wound. Dylan cleared his throat and fidgeted with the faucet.

"What? No!" Her cheeks turned a shade darker, and she stabbed her innocent pancake with her fork. I knew saying her ex-boyfriend's name wouldn't go over easily, but I couldn't help myself. I wanted her, and now that she was single, I had a shot. Plus, I wondered what else got her flustered.

Cora huffed and stood. Pushing her empty plate away, she held my gaze. The fire in her eyes was imminent. She grabbed the other girl's hand and dragged her out of the kitchen.

"Well, you managed to piss Cora off. Good job." Dylan's response was snarky, no surprise, though.

I plopped down onto a stool and snatched a plum from the fruit basket in front of me. "She's a teenager. She'll get over it. How old is she?"

"Nineteen, and she's a complete riot."

"Like father like daughter, right?"

His gaze bounced from one side of the kitchen to the next as a beat of silence strained between us.

"So, are you here to give me an ear full?"

He swirled his coffee around in his cup as he waited for my answer. I took another bite out of the plum as I observed the feminine decor of his kitchen. "As much as I want to tell you how stupid your plan was, I'll keep it to myself, but no, I'm not here to give you an ear full." I swallowed and waited for his reply. Dylan had always been an easy-going guy, but forgiveness wasn't one of his strong suits.

He rubbed the back of his neck. The pinch of unhappiness in his face was evident. "Well, I guess you got to witness my life turn to shit once again."

I leaned onto the island and knocked my knuckles against the white marble. "I wanted to tell you yesterday that I'm selling my dad's house. I won't have much of a reason to come back. Thought I should tell you in person."

His brows jogged up his forehead, and he turned, tossing his mug into the sink before reaching for the fridge handle. A row of bottles rattled on the side of the door, and he grabbed a beer, but only one. He never drank before 4 PM, so I knew the breakup was doing a number on his heart, even if he hid his emotions behind a static glare.

"Look, I know you blame me for severing our friendship, but it wasn't intentional. You had life shit going on and Cora. What was I suppose—"

"Yeah, well, I had dreams too. Cora wasn't going to stay young forever. You could have waited, but you ran off with our ideas and pretended like they were your own," he said, cutting me off.

Before I could get another word out, he stormed out of the kitchen. I followed close behind until we were both standing in front of Cora's little green car. Cora's friend struggled as she loaded the trunk with all Cora's things. A wave of heat washed over me as I studied Cora's movements. Those big lips, soft skin, and perky breasts. She wasn't a little girl anymore, and I wanted to drag her out of that car and pin her to the hood. Dylan rounded the front of the car before stopping at the driver's side door.

"Who are you?" the tall blonde-haired girl asked as she walked over.

I folded my arms across my chest and locked my gaze back on Cora. "An old friend."

She popped her gum and twirled a golden lock around her finger. "Oh. Are you going to the cabin too?"

I quirked a brow. "The cabin?"

"Yeah. Cora's running away for the summer. She's going to hide out and become a cavewoman for a month or so. I don't blame her, honestly. I mean, if I caught my boyfriend titty fucking—"

"Alone?" I interjected her mid-sentence.

"Yup. Oh, don't worry, she prob won't make it three nights. She's scared of everything. She'll be back soon enough, and I'll have to listen to her cry about still being a virgin. Le sigh."

"Virgin?" I winged a brow.

She froze and a beat of silence followed. "Whoops. Don't tell her I said anything. Please," she begged.

I gave her a once over. "Your secret's safe with me."

She smiled and walked back over to the car and gave Dylan a fist bump and waved to Cora before getting into her luxury car.

A familiar feeling that I've long buried came bubbling to the surface, and all the important things that I needed to take care of suddenly went out the window. The only thing I cared about was making sure Cora got to the cabin safely and making sure she stayed there.

CHAPTER 7
Sexy Savor – Cora

I HAD FINALLY ESCAPED, later than I'd wanted but right when I was about to enter the highway, Emma called me and asked if I had packed my vibrator. I told her I could buy one online and have it delivered, but then I remembered it would probably take forever, and my dad would see the charge on the statements. *Gosh, I really need to get a separate checking account.* Finding a good reason to turn back around was hard enough. I hurried to my bedroom and tossed open the drawer, tossing aside the pile of thick sweaters to reveal a pair of pink silicone rabbit ears. Tucking it under my arm, I powered down the steps and out of the front door before my dad could stop me.

I SLOWED the car and exited the freeway as I looked for the grocery store. A bright yellow sign flickered above the flat building. I parked and grabbed a cart and started down the long empty aisles. I wasn't much of a cook, so frozen tv dinners and seltzer water was my only option. I roamed the store, making sure I picked up enough food to last me a few weeks or so. The only bad thing about chilling out in the middle of nowhere was the store wasn't just around the corner. Spotting the chilled Starbucks frappes, I grabbed a case of them and almost dropped it as my phone vibrated in my back pocket.

"Hey." I continue loading cases of Starbucks frappes into my cart before moving down the aisle.

"Did you make it?"

"Dad, I'm almost there. I had to make a stop for food. You don't want me starving in the woods, do you?"

He let out a low chuckle and then cleared his throat. "There's a bad storm on the way out there. You need to book it to the cabin asap."

I rolled my eyes and found a spot behind a lady with wild hair and shaggy slippers as I waited to check out. "I'm checking out now."

"Call me, or else I'll be sending a search party out for you," he scolded.

"I'm not a little girl anymore, Dad. You won't die if I don't call." I placed my groceries on the conveyer belt and winced as the loaf of bread became smashed between the two cases of seltzer.

We said our goodbyes, and minutes later, I was hauling ass back to my car when a slither of lightning crawled across the black sky. *Great.* I loaded the backseat, hoping to get everything inside before the soft rain turned into stinging bites of hell. Slamming the door shut, I rounded the car and hopped into the driver's seat. The road was clear, but the rain started to pick up, and my windshield wipers were no match for the golf ball-sized raindrops smashing against my car. *Fucking vibrator.*

I reached for my phone, nearly coming to my death as I almost collided with the railing. With my hands glued to the steering wheel, a sigh of relief washed over me when I spotted the sign for the road to the cabin. Only twenty more miles to go and I'll be in a nice warm bed with my snacks on one side of me and my book on the other. Silly me for thinking nothing else could go wrong. The lights on my dashboard lit up like a damn Christmas tree, and my car jolted before coming to a stop.

Screaming out loud would have been pointless, so I just slumped back in my seat. Reaching for my phone, I froze, refusing to call my dad because he would order a tow truck to bring me home, and calling Emma was out of the question. She was a terrible driver, and I was in no mood to hear her complain incessantly as we drove back home. I sucked in a breath and googled the nearest tow truck company when a pair of bright headlights lit up my back window, nearly blinding me.

Unable to see the person in the truck from my rearview mirror, I stepped out into the drenching rain. The person in the truck didn't get out, leaving me contemplating if I should get closer or get my ass back in my car and lock the door. Retreating a few feet, the driver-side door of the truck swung open, and a muscular man with wild dark-colored hair stepped into my bubble.

"Brett?"

Annoyance bubbled up inside me, although I was stuck in the middle of nowhere during a rainstorm, seeing Brett just agitated me more. The last thing I wanted was Brett to come to my rescue. Again.

"What are you doing here?" I took a step back and almost stepped out of my sandals.

I knew exactly how I looked in this moment. Like a drowned cat, but Brett looked like he was created to get wet. How could someone look like a Greek god in the middle of a thunderstorm? He stepped closer, and the toe of his boots grazed the toe of my sandal. Sheets of heavy raindrops surging down his face concealed his chocolate eyes.

"I could ask you the same thing. Car trouble?"

"Obviously," I deadpanned before folding my arms across my sodden chest.

A stiff grin played across his face, and my knees weakened. I hated him for making my body react in ways that it shouldn't. He was old enough to be my dad, but my body didn't care what I thought obviously.

A beat of silence stretched between us, and he walked away. He climbed back into his truck, and my shoulders slumped. Sure, I hated him, but damn I didn't think he'd leave me in the middle of the road with a broken-down car.

"Do you enjoy standing out in the rain, or are you gonna get in?"

"What about my stuff?" I yelled. The thought of leaving all my cases of Starbucks made me want to cry. I huffed and opened the back door. A cracking sound roared through the sky and made my heart drop in my stomach.

"Any day now," he yelled from the window.

Grabbing my backpack and a case of Starbucks, I slammed the door closed and hurried over to his open passenger side door. I placed my backpack and case of Starbucks on the floor and settled in the soft leather seat as he pulled off into the darkness.

CHAPTER 8
Stalking Tendencies ~ Brett

I WAS in luck when she'd had to turn around and go back for her vibrator. Cora's lime green hatchback pulled into the driveway. She didn't even notice me; she was too busy running up the steps toward her bedroom. By the time she reappeared, I was already in my truck, but the little hint of pink that peeked from under her arm was clear as day—*naughty little girl.*

My primal senses kicked in. Cora seemed sweet and innocent, but something deep down inside of me let me know there was more to this little mouse. She tossed the vibrator into her backpack and climbed back into the driver's seat. Pulling out like a madwoman on a mission, her tires screeched against the pavement, and I followed close behind.

I had never seen anyone drive as terrible as her before, and that was saying a lot. Living in California,

I've seen the worst of the worst, but Cora drove as if her eyes were glued shut. My body remained in a tense state the entire time I stayed behind her, and when she switched lanes without her blinker, it almost killed me. My big break came when she made a stop at the grocery store. Dylan would make sure Cora always had a safe and reliable car; that was the father in him. But I wasn't her father, I was daddy, and daddy always got what daddy wanted.

I popped the hood of her car and dislodged a few important components. Nothing that would make her crash, but she wouldn't get too far, and that's what I wanted. Then I waited.

"Were you following me?" she asked, her words dipped in accusation as she wrangled with her wet and now matted hair.

I kept my gaze on the open road, but the corner of my lip twitched with excitement. She fidgeted with her fingers before relaxing back into the seat. God, I wanted to eat her up. She looked a hot mess, but a delicious mess. Hints of her coconut scent wrapped around my nose, and her nipples pebbled in her bra. They were the perfect size. Easy to palm and stuff in my mouth. So soft and suckable.

"Maybe we are just headed to the same place," I said as I took a sip of water.

She glared at me before biting down on her bottom lip. "Which is where?"

"I'm headed to a little cabin in the woods. What about you?"

"What? No. No. No. I'm headed to the cabin. Alone. I need to be alone with my thoughts, and the last thing I need is another boy making me feel all...ugh."

"I'm not a boy, I'm a man and it's not healthy to fight it." I grinned.

"Fight what?" she asked in an icy tone.

"Your bodies reaction to our kiss the other day." I winked and tapped my thumb on the steering wheel as I waited for her to calm down. Her hands went limp, and she lowered her chin to her chest. She looked like the world was coming to an end, but she was wrong. So very wrong.

"Chin up, buttercup. You might actually like me after our stay."

"Uh. Our stay? The cabin is a one-bedroom with a shitty couch and an empty loft. Where are you going to sleep?"

My cock stirred at her feistiness. She had a mouth on her, and it killed me. I could shut her up with my cock. The thought of forcing my shaft down her shallow tiny throat made me squirt a stream of pre-cum in my boxers. Luckily, it was dark, and she couldn't see my cock begging to be whipped out of my pants.

She continued to babble on about how I ruined her

mini summer vacation, but she had no idea the things I had planned for her. I texted a buddy of mine who owned a tow company to pick up her car and take it back to his garage until I called for it. I wanted Cora all to myself, and I'll be damned if she tried to run off in the middle of the night.

"We can share the bed. It's big enough if I remember correctly," I said as I adjusted in my seat.

A scream of frustration broke past her plump lips, and I had to bite back a low moan. A ribbon of lust swirled in my core as I watched her go from mildly annoyed to full-blown agitated. Her back slammed into the leather, and her feet kicked the floor numerous times. Those full plump lips pouted, and her wet matted hair fell to the front of her face. My cock ached, my mouth watered, and my palm itched. Little girls who threw temper tantrums deserved to be spanked. Hard.

"My phone. We have to go back," she protested.

I shook my head and turned to meet her gaze. "If you forgot, it must not have been that important to you."

"I need my phone, or my dad will—"

I held up a hand, cutting her off. "I'll text Dylan and tell him you made it to the cabin."

"Oh yeah? You're going to tell the man that hates your guts that you kidnapped his only daughter and refused to go back for her phone? Good luck with that."

I pulled my bottom lip between my teeth and stroked my thumb across my stubbled chin. She had a point, Dylan and I weren't on good terms, but even so, I knew he would be thankful that I picked up Cora versus her being stranded on the side of the road.

"First of all, he doesn't hate me. We had a mutual misunderstanding, and second of all, I didn't kidnap you. You got in my truck all by yourself." I winked and returned my eyes to the ominous road in front of me.

We sat in silence for a few seconds, with only the faint sounds of country music and the raging storm outside filling the truck's cabin. I waited with bated breath for her next outburst. Hell, I anticipated it. Every slick word that flowed off her tongue sent a wave of electricity down my spine that ended at the tip of my swollen cock.

I wanted to hold her yet punish her at the same time. She was used to getting what she wanted—spoiled and entitled, with the word "no" being the key that unlocked her unruly childlike behavior. Bright lights stole her attention, and she locked her gaze on the large blue exit sign with a motel and fast-food symbol on it.

"Let me out. I don't want to go to the cabin. I'll call my dad and tell him to pick me up in the morning."

"Really?" I shrugged and switched lanes. My truck slowed as I entered the ramp and the sign for the shitty motel came into view. I drove up to the door and put my truck in park. "Have fun."

The whites of her eyes brightened, and her lips spread into a grim line. I knew she didn't want to go back home. The only thing waiting for her there was bad memories and her dad, who was probably going to spend the rest of the summer drowning his heartache in beer and working long hours. She returned her gaze to the flickering light on top of the motel and then focused on a couple of men who looked like something that nightmares were made of loitering outside by the snack machine. She wouldn't survive twenty minutes at this motel.

"Fine. But you're sleeping on the couch."

I winked and put the truck in drive. "Whatever floats your boat, baby girl."

CHAPTER 9
Good Girl, Bad Girl~Cora

STAYING at the motel wasn't an option. It looked like it was infested with rats and run by some low-life convict and his scary friends. I sucked in a breath and slumped back into the seat. Brett's irritating yet intoxicating smile shined through the darkness, and I rolled my eyes. We didn't speak for the rest of the ride, but he made it a point to get under my skin the entire way.

The small glances in my direction, where the flicker of light from the lightning in the sky bounced off his chocolate irises. The strong spider web of veins that ran under the toasted tanned skin of his hands. I tried to look away, but something about him had my eyes glued to his muscular frame. Even in the darkness of the truck, his body took up the entire seat. Forgetting about our little kiss was going to be a problem because the memory engraved itself on my brain. Everything about it was wrong, but for some odd reason, it felt so right. Our gazes locked, and my pulse staggered.

"Something on your mind, baby girl?" His voice reminded me of silk dipped in trouble. Smooth, deep, and dangerous.

I pressed my palms into my arms and shook my head. He refused to break his stare, looking at me like I was some sort of dessert. He slowed the truck and started down the dirt road toward the cabin. Memories resurfaced and a wave of nostalgia rolled off my shoulders. The cabin had always been my second home, and I'd spent my days sitting at the lake while dad made sandwiches and waited for me to come in to scarf them down like I hadn't eaten in years.

Layers of dead pine needles crunched under the truck's weight, and the worn oak logs of the cabin came into view. Forgetting for a split second that Brett would be joining me on my little vacation, I opened the door and made sure to slam it hard before walking to the front door.

"Doors locked," he yelled.

I stopped in my tracks and turned around slowly before popping my hip out. "Let me guess. You have a key to?"

An annoying and even more titillating smile crawled across his lips, and he pulled my backpack from the front seat. "Nope. I just use the one under the mat." His eyes cascaded in the direction of my feet, and I bent down, rolling one corner of the mat to reveal a small key.

"I didn't know he left one here."

"He didn't. I did. You know your dad thinks the world is too full of shit people with bad intentions to leave a key under the welcome mat."

"Can you blame him?"

He shrugged and placed my backpack near my feet. "It depends on what you consider bad intentions."

I let his words flow in one ear and out the other and opened the door. I wrinkled my nose at the musty earth smell that lingered in the air. The cabin was cool, dark, and depressing. *Ugh. I guess I should have stayed home.*

I stepped further inside and stood in the middle of the small room. I didn't remember it being this small, or maybe it just seemed that way because I had an uninvited guest. I circled the living room and entered the kitchen. A light covering of dust settled on the countertops, and I swiped my finger across it. Brett's heavy footsteps smashed the dead leaves with each step, and the sliver of light illuminating from his truck vanished, leaving me in pitch blackness.

"Thanks a lot," I yelled.

"For what?" He flicked on the living room light, and a warm hue lit the small space. He dropped his bags to the floor, and my shoulders jumped at the thump.

He toed off his dirty boots and placed them on the shoe tray near the door. I stood behind the center island, observing every flex his bulging muscles made as he rearranged his things. The man was made of steel, and no amount of clothing could hide that. The stiff denim of his jeans stretched across his trunk-like thighs as he kneeled. I never paid attention to older guys, even ones only a few years older than me. Emma liked them seasoned, or whatever she called the ones old enough to be her dad. I always avoided the conversation when she started to veer off into old man territory. I always thought Josh was the one for me until I found out he wasn't.

I swirled around and pried open the fridge door. Three empty shelves and a pile of expired ketchup packets greeted me. "Ugh."

"Hungry?" He walked over to the fridge, his steps slow and steady.

I took a step back and leaned against the center island. "We have no food. All the food was in my car, the one that you left behind." I twirled a lock of hair around my finger and crossed one ankle over the other.

He raised his hands. "I have food."

"What? Why?"

His back met my gaze as he walked over to the

door where his pile of bags sat. Grabbing two large grey totes, he carried them over and set them on the center island. "Why? Because I had no plans of starving while here."

He unzipped the first bag, retrieving fruits, vegetables, cheese, and other yummy contraband that I wanted to shove past my lips in an act of desperation.

I grabbed the loaf of brioche bread and leaned in. "What is this? The Mary Poppins bag of food?"

He pulled out a few more items and then placed the bag on the floor. "No, it's just a big bag, baby."

My stomach tightened at his words. *Baby*. I couldn't remember the last time someone else called me baby, but apparently, I liked it. He brought the other large grey bag and set it down on the center island.

"Do the honors," he said as he slid it over toward me.

Hesitation set in and I gave him an odd stare before lowering my gaze into the bag. My fingers tingled at the sights before me, and I pulled out the contents. A bag full of my favorites. Starbucks frappes, strawberry licorice, mini cupcakes, and other yummy goodies I couldn't bear to live without. My attention was so hard set on the snacks below my eyes that I hadn't noticed the heat from his warm breath on the back of my neck.

"D—did you get all this for me?" My words came

out muddled, and I swallowed down the lump in my throat.

He leaned in some more and wrapped my matted tresses around his fist, forcing my chin toward the ceiling. "Yes, but you can't eat them just yet. You have to earn it."

His dangerous and unfamiliar words ruined the steady beat of my pulse. My limbs tingled, and my mouth watered, but the most shocking sensation of all was the throb coming from between my legs.

CHAPTER 10
Baby Girl Bath Time ~ Brett

GOD, she smelled so good. Her body tensed beside mine, and it only made my cock harder. I enjoyed how she tried to hold on to her innocence, but I saw her squeeze her legs together, which meant it was only a matter of time before I had her on her knees. I wanted to ruin every single inch of her body. A slight shiver ran down her spine, and I pressed into her back. I know she felt it. She had to.

My cock straining underneath the stiff denim, begging for something warm and tight. She had three holes, and every one of them was stamped with a V. It reminded me of Christmas. Her virgin body and my throbbing dick. She could run, but she couldn't hide. There was nowhere for her to go, and I made sure of that. I removed her hands from the bag of licorice and placed them behind her back.

I let my lips graze the shell of her ear. "Be a good girl and get ready to take a bath, and then maybe you can have a snack."

She tried to wither out of my grasp, but she was too weak. "I'm not a little girl. I can have a damn snack whenever I want to."

Her reluctance continued to send shockwaves through my veins, and I loved every minute of it. I pulled on her matted tresses and wrapped my arm around her plush belly. Forcing her body in the direction of the bathroom, I shoved her inside, and she turned, her cheeks spotted with red. My lip curled at the sight of her disobedience. Her chest rose and fell with each ragged breath, and I kneeled beside the clawfoot tub.

"Take your clothes off, baby girl."

"No," she spat.

I gave her a once over and pumped a few drops of body wash into the warm water. She stood; hands folded across her chest with her lips pouted. *How fucking cute.*

"I promise you, you don't want to say no to me." I stood and closed the space between us until my chest pressed against the softness of her breasts.

Her brain contemplated as she chewed the inside of her cheek. With an unyielding gaze, she finally gave in and dropped her arms. Her eyes drifted away from mine and landed on the tub. Slowly and reluctantly, she tore at her damp clothing. The straps of her tank top slid down her soft arms, exposing her little pink bra. My tongue slithered across my bottom lip at the anticipation of seeing her pebbled rosebud nipples.

I followed her movements, her dainty fingers fidgeting with the zipper of her shorts. She drew in a breath and then released it as she shimmied out of them. I couldn't have severe the line of my gaze on her deliciously plump body if I'd wanted to. I eased in some more until my breath ruffled the loose strands of hair near her forehead. She stood before me in a pink bra and pink cotton panties.

"Keep going?" I whispered in her ear.

Every curve on her plush body made my skin sizzle. She was perfect in every way, although she tried to hide from me. Hips thicker than honey and a belly softer than a cloud with a highway of stretch marks. She had no idea how crazy I was about her at this exact moment. The cups of her bra loosened and floated to the floor. Hard pebbles greeted me, and I placed my thumbs to them. She whimpered, her big eyes fluttered, and I hooked my thumbs underneath the waistband of her panties and yanked them down.

"Mmm, a juicy pretty pussy for a juicy little girl," I teased as I kneeled below her.

A wave of color whooshed up her neck at my words. I wondered if they made her uncomfortable, but honestly, I didn't care. I wanted her to hear all the filthy dirty things that ran rampant in my mind before I made her feel them. I picked her up, and she yelped. The water was warm to the touch, and I lowered her into the tub. Her posture relaxed once she got settled, and I grabbed a soft washcloth from the small closet adjacent to the tub and kneeled beside her.

"Are you going to be a good girl and let daddy make you all clean?"

She nodded and leaned back. The tub was half full, with just enough bubbles. I wanted to see her wet body through the water. I spread her legs and dragged the wet washcloth up her thigh. Her flesh came alive with an army of goose bumps littering her delicate skin. Her suckable nipples teased me as the water played peek-a-boo with each movement I made. I repeated my actions, taunting her with the washcloth as I trailed up and around every inch of her body. Lust crept into her features, but she tried to hide it. I had every intention of unlocking her dirtiest desires because good girls needed to be punished.

"Do you still want to go home?" I asked.

She shook her head, and I made my way behind her. Grabbing the bottle of shampoo off the shelf, I dumped some into my hand and lathered her raven-colored tresses. My fingers massaged her scalp, and she moaned at the sensation.

I loosened the belt to my jeans and let the rasp of the zipper stretch between us. Her motions stilled, and it just made my dick throb harder. My lips found the shell of her ear, and I slithered my tongue inside. She clenched her legs and held her breath.

"I almost forgot, you were a bad girl today. That little stunt you pulled on the drive up. Tsk Tsk. Now—"

"What? I didn't mean—" she interrupted, her words catching in her throat.

"Shh. I know. You were pissed that I ruined your plans, but naughty girls must be disciplined. Right?"

She hesitated for a moment and then nodded.

"Good, because daddy's going to take your mouth tonight and your pussy tomorrow."

CHAPTER 11
His Salty Seed - Cora

A TINGLE RAN down my back at his dark words. Josh never talked to me the way Brett had. It was wrong, filthy, dirty but also very hot. I shouldn't like it, and I shouldn't want to crawl into bed with someone who was old enough to be my dad, but damn, Brett was making it hard for me to say no, and the constant throb from my most sensitive spot wasn't helping. I never believed in fate, but just as my life had gone to shit, Brett was there to console me.

To my surprise, his touch was soft, yet the calloused pads of his finger made my body come to life. It was like he could see through my soul and my flaws but didn't care about any of it. The rumble of the water draining stole my attention, and Brett stood.

I hadn't noticed that he removed his shirt and slabs of riveting muscle stared me in the face. My eyes started at the bulge of his pecs and descended until I got to the waistband of his boxers. Curly hairs peeked over the band, and I slid my tongue between my lips as I got to my feet. He wrapped me up in a large white towel, and I climbed out of the tub.

Picking me up, he carried me to the bedroom and dropped me down in front of the bed. His touch made my skin sizzle, and I hated it but craved it at the same time. I wondered if Brett could be my little secret, and no one had to know about us or all the things he would do to me. I couldn't face my father if he knew I fucked his best friend, even if they weren't really on speaking terms.

I wouldn't be able to face him at all. The air in the bedroom was stale just like the rest of the cabin. Brett tugged at my towel and it dropped to the carpet. The palms of his hand found my cheeks, and he pressed his lips on mine. Like a fire burning through my soul, his tongue thrashed against the insides of my mouth, and I wanted more. His kiss was hard and unforgiving. So much different than the kiss from yesterday. Chasing his mouth as he pulled away, he placed his hand on my stomach and held me in place. I worked my tongue over my thirsty lips, a subtle beg for his to return to mine. But instead, he made me suffer and forced his thumb past my lips.

"On your knees, little mouse."

I lowered to my knees and placed my arms over my belly.

"Daddy's going to teach you a new skill." A smile darker than the devils danced across his face.

I lowered to my knees and sat back on my ankles. With my dampened lips still wrapped around his thumb, he retrieved it and teased me as he tucked both of his thumbs under his waistband. His towering height forced my chin to the ceiling, and a sly grin crawled across his lips.

"Keep those lips parted for daddy. You'll be pacifying on something much bigger in just a minute."

In one swift movement, he removed his jeans and then his boxers.

A violent bulging piece of flesh that leaked at the tip hung inches from my lips. I shrank back. Staring at it made a wave of heat warm my blood.

Veins that reminded me of highways zigzagged around the shaft of his flesh, starting at the base and ending at the tip. He inclined, making sure the bulb hovered in front of my lips. He leaked one drop and then another. I've never done this before, but I wanted to. I swallowed and placed my hands on his muscular thighs. His powerful hand fisted my locks, sealing my fate, and he pushed his hips forward. I choked, my words catching in my throat, with the taste of his salty seed on my tongue.

"Just like a lollipop. All suction and no teeth," he said, his breath catching in his throat. Without a chance to swallow, he shoved it all the way back and waited until my fingers clawed at his skin as I begged for air. I gulped the air once he pulled out, sucking in as much as I could, but he didn't leave me enough time to fill my lungs before forceful gurgles and bubbling drool crept off my bottom lip.

He fed me his flesh until it disappeared down my tiny throat. I sucked hard as I kept my teeth away from his pulsating cock. His facial expressions were like a rainbow of emotion, each expression more pronounced than the last. His calloused hands found mine, and he removed them, holding them down at my side as he made my mouth his dumpster. My sloppy wet sucking sounds pierced the air and ripped the veil of silence that cloaked it. His cock was a choking hazard, and he made sure I choked good and well.

"You're such a fucking good girl. Goddamn." His voice was rugged and hard but still had a taint of softness.

One more hard tug on my hair and his hips jolted. With our gazes locked, he let his flesh pulsate and a steady stream of salty goodness dripped down my throat like raw honey. He made sure I swallowed it all as he rubbed a calloused thumb down my throat. With the deed done, he crooked a finger, and I rose to my feet.

His chocolate eyes turned a shade darker as he looked at me and it made my insides pirouette. It was an odd feeling, but I liked it. The prolonged stare, the ticking of his jaw as he bit down on his back molars, and the continued pulse of his hard cock. I pressed my lips together and tasted the last drops of his seed that settled on my bottom lip.

Twirling damp pieces of hair around my finger, I lowered my chin. "Can I get a snack now?"

He nodded and pointed to the bed. I walked over to the side as he pulled back the covers and climbed in. He placed a hand on my butt as he helped me onto the large bed. My body sank into the plush mattress, and he pulled the covers up to my chin. I never remembered the bed being this soft, but it had me struggling to keep my eyes open.

"Warm milk and cookies, and then off to sleep," he said before placing a kiss on my forehead.

I tracked his movements across the room and reached over to the small table beside me. Yanking open the drawer, I retrieved my coloring book and colored pencils.

CHAPTER 12
Sweet Nectar - Brett

SHE SLEPT like a baby last night, and I watched her all night. I laced her warm milk with a heavy sedative. I wanted her to have a goodnight's rest, but I also wanted to explore her body without interruption. She devoured the sweet cookies and then washed down the warm milk. Her eyes became heavy after a while, and I pushed her shoulders down into the mattress.

A yawn slipped off her yummy lips, and she fell into a deep sleep. Naked and unbothered, her chest rose and fell with each breath. She looked like a pure angel, although she was anything but. I was pinning with jealousy. My parched tongue cleaved to the roof of my mouth as I surveyed her curvy body below me. Pulling back the covers that hid her delectable frame, a drop of saliva escaped my lips, falling onto her belly button.

A soft whimper pushed past her lips, and her dainty fingers flinched. My name, in broken pieces, uttered off her tongue, and my lips curled into a devilish grin. She even slept like a baby. Her arms are on either side of her head with palms to ceiling and legs slightly spread. For a split second, it felt wrong, hovering over her like a sick pervert, but the feeling passed as I gently lowered my lips above the landing strip of hair above her sweet pussy.

She smelled divine, and I could only imagine how good she tasted. I separated her thighs with steady hands, careful not to wake her. Although the sedatives were potent, there was a small percentage of people that they didn't affect. I hoped she wasn't one of them. The sight of her pretty little cunt made my cock rise, and I wanted nothing more than to fuck her little brains out, but I wanted her to be awake for that so she could witness the theft of her cherry. Another seepage of breath left her lips, and a low moan followed. She twisted her body, turned on her stomach, and placed her tender, juicy ass right in my line of sight. I became hungry at that exact moment, and my hands found their rightful place on her tender flesh as I stretched them apart.

My parched tongue slipped between her folds, and her scent danced on my tongue. I told myself I would be gentle, go slow and enjoy the moment but all that went out the window once her candied juices dripped onto my lips. She wiggled, faint whimpers breaking the silence. Her subconscious tried to force her out of the coma-like sleep, but it was no use. I would devour her until lances of sunlight peered through the dusty blinds or until she came on my tongue.

My tongue flicked and twirled around her clit, and her body loved it. Curled toes, tense limbs, and low moans let me know I was driving her over the edge. The thunderstorms that tore open the sky eventually subsided, leaving behind the wet sucking sounds of my lips pacifying her swollen nub.

My hunger intensified when she arched her back, lifting her ass as she let out a strained whimper. I released my grip and slid two fingers inside. I nearly came at that moment. She wanted to be fucked. She was ripe and ready. Her virgin cunt begged to be taken, but not tonight. It couldn't be tonight. She clamped down around my fingers like a vice, sending a small trail of pre-cum flowing off the edge of my cock. I retrieved my fingers, now sticky with her sap. I continued my feast, my cruel tongue devouring her like an animal that hadn't eaten in days. Her whimpers, along with her movements, stilled, and then her body seized in my grasp. I was sure she would wake to find me tongue fucking her, but her eyes remained closed, and I stilled my movements until her muscles relaxed. My name dribbled off her lips, and I crawled to her, placing a soft kiss on her cheek.

I SIPPED on the hot cup of coffee as I waited for my naughty little girl to come into the kitchen. I didn't get a wink of sleep last night. After eating her pussy, I cleaned her up and placed the covers back over her. But my dick was rock hard, and it wouldn't back down until I gave it what it wanted. A few strokes with my closed fist, and I came hard. By the time I got settled in bed, it was already 5 AM. The sleeping sedatives had most likely worn off, so I waited with bated breath for her to appear.

A rush of excitement skated down my spine, but the little devil on my shoulder made sure to nudge me. A small part of me second guess my actions, made me wonder if what I did was wrong. I toyed with that fact and scrubbed my hands down my face. Was it wrong? She was nineteen and my ex-best friend's daughter. I took another sip of my coffee before setting the cup down on the center island.

But then again, there was so much woman to her, and that's what I wanted to explore. Albeit young, she housed a salacious temptress behind that good girl act, and I wanted to be the one to bring it out of her. Cora was forbidden fruit, and I craved a taste. I wanted every piece of her. She was mine the moment I laid eyes on her at the cookout, and she'll be mine forever. The wood creaked under her footsteps, giving her approach away.

"Morning, sunshine," I said as I pulled a rusty skillet from the island cabinet.

She stopped in the middle of the kitchen; confusion etched into her features. My blood slowed to a trek as I waited for her to speak.

"Where's my clothes?"

I pasted on a smile then cracked an egg into the sizzling skillet. "Why do you need clothes? Are you cold, baby?"

"Umm." She looked down at the outfit she was wearing.

I did the honors of rummaging through her things when she was asleep. Her backpack didn't have much clothing in it besides a few tops and an extra pair of shorts. I dumped everything out, and two extra pairs of white panties fell out of the bottom. Packing everything back up except her panties and tops, I placed her backpack in a closet and left her two articles of clothing on the edge of the bed.

I pulled a plate from the cabinet and set it next to the skillet as I waited for her bacon to finish burning to a respectable crisp. Just like God intended.

"Hungry?"

Her shoulders slumped, and she made her way to the small round kitchen table and sat down. Tossing her long raven locks out of the way, she waited, her fingers tapping the table in anticipation. "Are you cooking breakfast or burning it?"

I ejected the toast from the toaster and tossed it in the garbage before walking over to the table. "That mouth's going to get you in trouble. Eat up."

"Kind of like your mouth?" She picked up a piece of bacon and slipped it past her lips as she held my gaze.

Fuck.

CHAPTER 13
Eggs and Bacon ~ Cora

I'D WOKE to tender folds and an overly sensitive clit. For a moment, I'd thought I had been dreaming. But it wasn't until that familiar rush, a wave of tingling nerve ends in my most sensitive spot going off like whistles as my climax approached. That's when I had awakened, right at the brink, and the only noise that escaped my lips was a cry of pleasure that not even my trusty vibrator was able to give me.

Once my legs were released, and the wave of ecstasy died, a ribbon of shame engulfed me. I'd kept my eyes closed, although I died to open them. My brain wouldn't let me fall back asleep, so I'd laid there with closed eyes and open ears. Taking in the primal grunts that echoed off the bathroom walls as he stroked his monstrous cock. Sounds that should have had guilt consuming me from within did the exact opposite. I'd liked it, the low growls as he reached his peak. It was wrong to want a man old enough to be my father, but as each hour passed, I craved more of his touch. I craved more of him.

"Don't think too hard. You might blow a brain cell," he teased.

I rolled my eyes and stabbed my fork into the crispy bacon before picking it up. "Why? Would blowing a brain cell impact me blowing something else?"

I winced as the legs of the worn wooden chair scratched against the oak floor. Bringing the coffee back to his lips, which were hidden behind two-week-old stubble, he took another sip, winging a brow as he locked his gaze on mine.

"That's the beauty of fucking baby girl. It's all primal. No brains required."

My flesh tingled at his words. *Baby girl.* His features were even more distinctive in the daylight. Chestnut hair that fell perfectly in his face, with a chiseled jaw and chocolate eyes that anyone could get lost in. A soft grey colored t-shirt covered his wall of muscle that stretched over his veiny biceps.

"You're doing it again…" His words trailed off as he picked up my fork.

My lips parted as he slid the fork carrying fluffy eggs into my mouth. The buttery yet salty taste dissolved on my tongue, and I swallowed. "Doing what?" I sliced my eyes back to my plate, playing with the pile of hash browns that were slowly turning cold.

"Spill it. Or I'm going to throw you over my shoulder and spank it out of you," he said as he shoved eggs past his lips.

"Just wondering why I wasn't good enough, you know? Like we were together since the beginning of high school. Everyone thought we were perfect together, and we had it all planned out—"

"Can't plan life. Sorry to break it to you, baby girl."

"But I need to know why I wasn't good enough."

"Do you? Why?" He scooped some more eggs on my fork and waited for my mouth to open.

I chewed with caution, rummaging my brain for an answer to his question. I always thought I'd be the one to dump someone, not the one being cheated and dumped on.

I placed my elbows on the table and pressed my palms into my cheek. "So, I can fix whatever turned him off."

He crooked a finger, urging me to come closer. Even with the aromas of bacon and salty eggs lingering between us, I still caught a whiff of his masculine scent. It was earthy, with hints of leather. I leaned in until our lips were inches from each other.

"Last time I checked, you weren't the problem." He placed a kiss on my cheek and stood, grabbing my plate before walking over to the sink.

I didn't need a mirror to know my cheeks were now a shade darker, the heat flowing through my body was evident. The sea of muscle rippled with each movement as he cleaned, and I finally snatched my gaze away when a mischievous grin played across his lips.

He cleared his throat and wiped his hands on the raggedy towel that lay over his shoulder. "Are you ready, baby?"

Like a deer in headlights, I came to a blank, my mouth creeping open only for jumbled syllables to crash on the edge of my tongue. "Um, uh...we'll..." I leaned back in the chair and blew out a breath.

Tilting his chin to the ceiling, he finished off the last of his coffee and put the cup into the basin of soapy water before sauntering over to me. Taking my hand in his, he kneeled between my legs and locked his gaze on me. "I have no plans of letting you go, Cora. I want you, all of you, and I don't give a damn about what your dad might think."

"He won't let me be with you. He'll probably kill you and disown me. Plus, I'm young and inexperienced in all things adult, and—"

"You need to give yourself more credit. If it wasn't for you, Dylan would have walked off a cliff by now. You're the glue keeping everything in his life together. His schedule, the house, the bills..." His words trailed off, and I ran my fingers over the grooves of his watch.

"How do you know that? Are you a low-key stalker?" I joked.

He kept his expression neutral. "Dylan might hate my guts, but he didn't block me on Facebook yet, so. He makes posts about you all the time. FYI." He brushed his thumb over the corner of my mouth, wiping away the leftover eggs. "Josh did you a favor because if he hadn't cheated, I would be on my way back to California right now."

"Oh…" I let my words trail off and blew out a breath. "I can't believe I was saving myself for that jerk. I just feel so…"

Before I could finish my sentence, his lips were locked on mine, and for some odd reason, it was a perfect fit. I noticed each kiss was becoming stronger than the next, more soul-sucking, more intense, more intoxicating.

He pulled away, and my fingers grabbed at the soft fabric of his shirt. "I'm happy you saved yourself because I'm going to ruin you over and over again."

He stood and tugged at the hem of his shirt before pulling it over his head, revealing his wall of taunting Olympian washboard abs. He let his t-shirt drop to the floor. His darkened eyes and wet lips chilled my soul. His footsteps were heavy and slow. He circled me and made my pulse stagger. I swallowed and stilled my movements. He pulled the other chair in front of me and held my gaze as he lowered himself onto it. He tapped his palm against his thigh, with wet lips and spread legs.

He cocked his head. "Come here."

"You want me to sit on your lap?".

A wave of heat brewed in my core, not knowing what Brett had planned for me. He looked at me with hunger in his eyes, and a small part of me hoped I could curb his hunger. I got up and took a small step, his hands landed on my waist, tugging me forward. He slipped his fingers under the waistband of my panties, and the muscles in his arms flexed as he tore them to shreds. Out of habit, I shielded myself, and he blocked my action and forced my arms back to my side.

"Stop it." The strength of his palms sent a wave of electricity zipping down my spine.

I pulled my bottom lip between my teeth. "Stop what?"

"No. You call me daddy."

"Daddy?" I licked my lips and sliced my eyes to the checkered dishcloth hanging off the edge of the table.

A cunning smile tugged at the corner of his mouth. "Yes?"

My knees turned to jelly at the octave drop in his voice. Dark was an understatement. It reminded me of a smooth baritone dipped in lust and wrapped in obsession.

"Stop what, Daddy…" I let my words trail off as I returned my gaze to the comfort of the torn rag on the table.

Blood rushed to my wrist once his grip loosened, and he clipped his finger under my chin. "Hiding yourself. You can't hide from me, little mouse. You're mine, every single beautiful curve of your body." Heat warmed my cheeks, and a dollop of wetness settled between my thighs. He stood and forced me to take a step back before tugging me toward the large couch. Making himself comfortable, he settled in, spreading his trunk-like legs so that the tight denim of his jeans strangled across them.

"Come to daddy." His tongue slithered across his bottom lip, and he placed his hands on my hip. I yelped as he swung me across his lap. He lifted his feet on the solid wooden coffee table, which consequently rose my ass high in the air.

I strained my neck, so our gazes met. "Are you going to spank me?" My words came out raspy, and I swallowed down the extra saliva filling my mouth.

He caressed my ass before letting his hand rest on my lower back. "Yes, because you're a naughty girl and naughty girls get spankings before they're fucked good and hard."

Before I could ask any more questions, a light sting spread across my ass cheeks. I really didn't know how to describe it. It was a mix of pleasure, with only a drop of pain, but I wanted more. He eyed my movements with each smack, and I felt myself purposely lifting my ass. His smacks became harder, and the sting from his palm eventually evaporated.

"A pretty red bottom for a pretty virgin girl," he said before sitting me up.

He raised one arm above his head and leaned into the couch. We sat in silence for a small beat, and I fought the urge to look behind me.

"Turn around and look." He gestured.

I turned and examined my very red bottom from the tall mirror adjacent to me. I ran a finger over the warmed skin, and it tingled, but I enjoyed the feeling. I enjoyed Brett. When I sliced my eyes back to him, he was completely naked, legs wide and cock standing at attention. His eyes ate me up as he stroked his length, his gaze was unyielding.

He removed a small purple bottle from the other side of him and squeezed a sizable amount of lube onto the tip of his oozing cock. "Are you ready?"

I nodded and started to lean back, but he shook his head and reached for my hand. "Umm...I..."

"You are so fucking beautiful that it nearly kills me, and tonight you're going to ride daddy's cock so I can cement every fucking facial expression you make into my brain."

His husky voice had my body breaking out in goose bumps. He pulled my arm and positioned my thick thighs over his strong ones. No longer at eye level, I looked down at him, my breasts inches from his lips, and he pulled a pebbled nipple into his mouth. His dagger-like tongue brought my body to life, and I craved it, especially my clit. Taking turns between each nipple, his mouth was the devil, and I was spellbound. A low moan escaped my lips as he withdrew his mouth, and a trail of saliva followed.

Pulling me into his chest, his lips found the shell of my ear. "Your first moans will be from pain, but I promise to have you screaming in pleasure."

His words destroyed me, and he hadn't even fucked me yet. Sealing my fate, he adjusted, lining up the head of his flesh to my entrance. A slither of fear settled in my chest when I realized how small my hole was and how big his cock was. Grabbing onto my hips, he lowered me, and my muscles flexed. My hands found his hard chest, and I pressed into it.

"Such a fucking good girl. That's it, let daddy in." He slammed his head back against the couch as my folds devoured him.

Trying to resist his motions as I slowly adjusted to his size, I shut my eyes and bit down on my bottom lip. His fingers were like barbed wire and kept me in place. I froze and drew in a breath before opening my eyes. "It hurts. You're so big compared to my vibrator," I said in a whimper.

"I know, baby, but we're almost there. I promise."

He lowered me another inch until my lips devoured his entire length.

The pain soon subsided, and a fullness took its place. I leaned forward, and his arm snaked around my back. With our foreheads molded together, he took two scoops of my ass into his hands and lifted them. Emptying me out, I gasped, and then a moan ripped between my lips once he filled me back up. He did it over and over, and each time felt better than the last. Stopping to pull my vibrator from the folds of the couch, he placed it in my hand, and I lowered it to my clit. It buzzed violently He fucked me as if I weighed nothing, and I loved it. Ramming into me hard with each thrust, the sucking sounds of his cock filling me up filled the cabin.

"Is daddy fucking you good and hard? Are you daddy's little cum dumpster?"

I moaned and tossed my chin to the ceiling. The vibrator was tearing me to pleasurable shreds as I reached ecstasy. His hands found my throat, and he squeezed. Broken words lined up on the tip of my tongue, and my mouth parted with anticipation high on my tail.

Fucking me like there was no tomorrow, a sting radiated down my cheek as his palm slapped my face, and he shoved his thumb past my lips. "Answer me."

I nodded, and he shoved his thumb back further until the only thing I could do was pacify it. Low groans dribbled off his lips, and my body clenched. He removed his thumb and forced my face into the nape of his neck. Spasms took over my entire body, and then he stilled. A groan from the depth of salacious hell seeped into my ears, and along with it, a thick steady stream of his seed gushed into my channel. He pulsated, soaking my channel as his milk soothed the bite of pain that lingered. I let my body melt into his, heat surrounding us as our ragged breaths heaved off our lips. The air was thick with summer heat and fresh sex. He combed through my tresses, massaging my scalp, and I lifted my gaze to his.

"Fuck, I love you," he whispered.

His words caught me off guard, sending my heart into a frenzy, one that I happily welcomed.

CHAPTER 14
Taking Her V Card ~ Brett

IMPALING her sweet virgin pussy was the best feeling in the world and fuck... did I want to do it over and over again. My words caught her by surprise, but I couldn't swallow them down if I tried. She needed to know how I felt because I had no plans of giving her up. I had always loved Cora, but this love was different. This love was the kind that had you climbing mountains and giving it your all to make it work. She gave me the greatest gift of all, and she didn't even know it—the gift of trust.

My heart bloomed in my chest as shyness settled in her features. Her arms made their way to the center of her midsection, and I nipped at her to get her to remove them. She was all curves, thick thighs, and stretch marks. A complete work of art.

I carried her to the bathroom and planted her on

the floor. Running the bath didn't take long, and I grabbed a few towels from the closet.

"I can take a quick shower."

"Nonsense. Baby girls take baths," I said, stepping back inside. Dipping my hand in the water to make sure it was warm to the touch, I scooped Cora off the floor and placed her into the tub. I couldn't help but nuzzle my chin on top of her head as she played with the bubbles. She tilted her head, and a question lingered on the edge of her tongue.

"Yes?" I asked while running a knuckle down her velvet cheek.

She sliced her eyes from wall to wall before settling them back on the mountain of vanilla-scented bubbles in front of her. "Why aren't you married or anything like that?"

A thickness formed in my throat at her question. "I was married a long time ago, but…" I let my words trail off and ran the soft towel up and down her arm. "She broke my heart, and after that, I buried myself in my business."

"You sound like Dad." She relayed a soft smile and splashed a few bubbles in my direction. Rehashing those harsh memories had me swallowing hard. I told myself I wouldn't love again after having my heartbroken, but Cora called to me, and being with her felt like home even with the steep age difference. I splashed more bubbles in her direction, making sure to coat her cute little button nose. Her giggle made heat swarm through me. So sweet and innocent.

"And you sound like a brat. Be careful, or I'll have you back over my knee." She poked her tongue out, revving up my cock with her brat-like ways.

My phone vibrated on the sink counter, saving her from the beast in my pants. *Fuck.* I made my greeting as unenthusiastic as possible and held the phone to my ear and left the bathroom. I intended to have a few weeks here with Cora, but the reality of owning your own business meant having to drop everything at a moment's notice.

One of my employees rambled on about something I had to drop everything to deal with. The call ended, and I took slow, heavy steps back into the bathroom. Cora had climbed out and was now wrapped in a fluffy towel. Perched on the edge of the tub, she stretched one leg as she applied lotion. I leaned against the doorframe, soaking her up as her hands moved in circles over her delicious body.

"Who was that?" Her voice reminded me of an intoxicating nectar that I just couldn't resist.

I folded my arms across my chest and lifted an arm above my head. "Work shit that I have to attend to."

My words made her spine stiffen, and she chewed the inside of her cheek. Before she could utter another word, my lips found hers, and the bottle of lotion dropped to the floor.

"Do you have to leave?" she asked.

Drilling my gaze into hers, I cupped her cheeks and placed a soft kiss on her forehead. "I do, but I'm not leaving without you."

I pulled her from the bathroom and into the bedroom. She stood by the bed as she watched me grab her backpack from the closet. Her posture was firm, and her expression closed as her head filled with all the what-ifs that would soon come to light. I pulled a shirt over my head and teased a finger under her chin to urge her to get dressed. The day was still young, and if we left in a few hours, we could get back to the city before midnight. I loved Cora, and I refused to be without her. Unfortunately, we had a wave of reality waiting for us once we got back, and just thinking about it had the blood in my veins stalling.

I HAD to contain my urge to grab her and fuck her senseless, but we had to get back to the city. I left her to get everything packed up as I snatched the keys to my truck from the drawer in the kitchen island. Sliding in, I inhaled her lingering scent. I loved her scent. If I could bottle it and have it forever, I would. If I could pin her to a bed in a basement without coming off as a sick fuck, I would do that too.

The engine revved, and I backed out of the dirt-lined driveway. The skin on my arms molded to the leather seat, and beads of sweat formed on the back of my neck. Blinding rays of sunshine had me reaching for my shades, and I nestled them on the bridge of my nose.

The drive to my friend's garage took about thirty minutes. I pulled into the parking lot, the wheels crunching under the gravel. A car I didn't recognize was parked next to Frank's, and I peered through the office window before stepping out of my truck. Metallica blasted from the corner speaker in the garage, and my knock went unnoticed. Walking between two luxury cars suspended in the air, I stepped into Frank's line of sight.

He relayed a smirk and rolled from underneath the muscle car he was working on. "About time your ass showed up."

Rising slower than a sloth, he dusted off his withering knees and wiped his arthritic hands on the black terry towel.

"It's only been a day. Did you reconnect the cable?"

He nodded and yanked Cora's car keys from the wall in front of us. "Her groceries are probably shit, but I took care of the TV dinners. Hope you don't mind."

The door to his office opened, and a man I'd never seen before emerged. He was an almost spitting image of Frank, except a few inches taller and with a little bit more hair.

"Who's this?" I asked as I leaned into the counter.

Frank gave a faint chuckle and picked up the styrofoam cup behind him. "Brett, this is Al. Al this is Brett. He has a habit of stalking young girls and fucking up their cars, so they're stranded."

Al folded his arms across his chest and relayed a saggy smile. "Is that so? You like em' young too?"

"Is that a problem?" I waited for Al to answer, but he sliced his gaze to the greasy floor and shoved his hands into the front pockets of his jeans. "So, how do you know Frank?"

"He's my brother."

I winged a brow and shared a glance between the both of them. Their lips remained in a hard line, a beat of silence passing between the three of us before Frank let out a breath.

"Didn't know you had a brother."

"You never asked." He shrugged and took another sip from the cup. "Is your truck out front?"

I nodded, and he brushed past me. I've known Frank for over twenty years, and not once had he ever mentioned a brother. The only family he talked about was the one he lost ten years ago. His wife and son died in a freak car accident.

"Do you live and work around here?" I asked Al as I waited for Frank to hook up Cora's car to the back of my truck.

He pressed his lips into a fine line and tilted his head to the side. "No. I live in Chicago, and I own a bar. I spend my days listening to grown men whine. So, you fancy the young ones hmm?"

His words were tainted in skepticism, but before I could explain myself, Frank's voice rounded the corner. I thanked him and climbed back into my truck. Pausing to check the time on my dashboard, my mouth went dry. It was already an hour past noon, and although I had Cora all to myself for the next couple of hours as we drove back, the reality of facing Dylan made me want to vomit.

CHAPTER 15
Hard Truths – Cora

IT WAS like all the happiness that Brett embodied evaporated from his body when he took the heavy bags from my grasp. I walked through the small cabin once more and blew out my cheeks as I fidgeted with the key. *Some vacation this was.* We packed up, and the engine to his truck roared, leaving a cyclone of dust behind us as he sped down the dirt road.

His truck was strong enough to tow my little green goblin back, and I was thankful I didn't have to drive alone with my thoughts in shit traffic. Brett tried to calm his nerves, but his repeated tapping of the steering wheel wasn't helping. A magnifying glass wasn't needed to see the sweat trickling down the back of his neck. He had every reason to be nervous, but so did I. How did one tell their father that their best friend of thirty something years took their daughter's virginity? I nestled against the cool leather, nuzzling my head on the headrest. Brett kept his eyes on the road, shifting his body every so often.

"Geez, I thought I'd never get you to shut up." I twisted a strand of hair around my finger before sticking my tongue out in his direction. *Very child-like. Just like Daddy hated.*

"I'm just thinking, baby girl. Why? You worried?"

"What are you thinking about?" I pried as I folded my arms across my chest.

He teetered his head from side to side and revealed that dangerous grin. "Oh, ya know. Just picturing you on your knees holding on to your unicorn stuffed animal as you choke on my cock." His voice, an octave lower, almost as if he did it on purpose, made goose bumps break out across my body.

"I know that's not all you're thinking about," I pestered.

He cleared his throat and placed his hand on my thigh, giving it a gentle squeeze. "Maybe you're right."

Intertwining my fingers with his, I tracked the pad of my pointer finger over the highway of veins protruding from his skin. I've known Brett my whole life, but this was the first time I'd seen him in a vulnerable state. After he left town I stalked him on social media. The guy with the penthouse in downtown LA who had his pick of the ladies. The guy who always wore a sinister grin with a dash of swagger in his step. But in this moment, he wasn't that guy.

He was the man who took my virginity and showed me just how beautiful I was. He was the man who stole my heart in twenty-four hours, and I was determined to let him keep it.

"Dylan..." I squeezed his hand, forcing his eyes to mine.

He raised a brow, and the corner of his lip curled. "I don't think I've ever heard you call your dad by his first name."

"It's just a name." Shrugging, I tugged the water bottle out of the holder.

"Yeah. Well, I guess it's all good unless your name is Brett." A nervous chuckle oozed off his lips as he scratched the edge of his chin.

"Is Dy— I mean, Dad—is his reason for being mad at you a legit one?"

"What did Dylan—"

"I don't care what he told me all these years. What happened, Brett?" I interjected.

His brows jogged up his forehead, and his calloused fingers found the tip of my chin. "Did I say you could call me by my first name?" He leaned in, his intense chocolatey gaze twisting my insides and commanding my focus on him.

I shook my head and dropped my stare to my lap.

"What's my name?"

I licked my lips before answering. Something about making him work for it sent a shiver crawling down my spine. "Trying to change the subject?"

A sly laugh rolled off his tongue, and his chest deflated. "Can we at least eat over it?"

I dangled my legs in the seat and clasped my hands together. "Sure… Daddy."

My words rippled the muscles in his jaw, forcing them to harden along with his cock. We pulled into a fast-food restaurant, and my stomach grumbled as fresh grease seeped into my nostrils. I stole a glance at the dashboard. We'd be pulling into my driveway soon.

THE REST of the ride home was dipped in silence. Brett told me what happened between him and my dad all those years ago, and just replaying the conversation in my head cast a heaviness on my shoulders. My dad had always been stubborn, but Brett wasn't any better, in all honesty. They were both pig-headed and bone-headed when they wanted to be, and dad couldn't relay his emotions if someone paid him a million dollars to do so.

Once the truck slowed and exited the freeway, my

limbs became a flighty mess. I couldn't remember the last time I'd been this nervous, but I'm sure Brett felt the same way. As the truck inched closer to my street, my heart sank into my stomach. As much as I wished for him to be passed out on the couch, the kitchen light let me know he was probably just getting around to his dinner as we pulled into the driveway. Although both of us were sitting on pins and needles, it became real once Brett killed the engine.

"Ready?" Brett asked as he pushed the door open.

I tugged at the handle and hopped down. He walked to the back of his truck to unhitch my car, leaving me to face the shaggy-haired man leaning in the doorway all by myself.

"Dad," I said, waving in his direction.

His brows hitched to the center of his forehead, and he took a swig of his beer. Keeping his gaze locked on mine until I stood inches from him. "Back so soon? What happened?" He reached out and tucked a lock of hair behind my ear.

A mountain of words piled on the edge of my tongue, but before they could drop off, Brett approached from behind. A beat of silence stretched between us before Brett cleared his throat.

"Can we have a word?" He shoved his hand into his front pocket and rocked on the heels of his boots.

Dad's eyes tightened at the corners, and he stood upright as he sliced his gaze between the both of us. I inhaled before vomiting the words he didn't want to hear out in the open.

"Excuse me?" He choked out before following my movements. "What do you mean you're moving to California with Brett? Am I missing something?"

With heavy footsteps, I charged to the kitchen in need of some chocolate and pistachio ice cream to weather this shit storm. Rummaging through the cabinets, I snatched the chocolate and tore it open. The lingering scents of beer seeped off my dad's breath, and I gave him an unyielding side-eye.

As if he just saw a ghost, all the color drained from his face, and he took a step back, and then another until his lower back slammed into the sink. I didn't want him to hate me over a decision my heart made, but the look in his eyes made me believe he'd probably hate me forever.

"Is that why you really went to the cabin? So you could—"

"No. Not at all," Brett interrupted before my dad could finish his sentence and I was grateful.

A laugh rippled through my dad's throat, and he raked his fingers through his greasy hair. It had only been twenty-four hours, but God, he looked like shit. Long hours, paired with a suddenly broken heart, was not a good look. I set the chocolate down and turned to walk over to him. Placing my small hands into his, I lowered my chin to his shoulder.

"Yeah, like I'll ever believe anything you have to say."

"I love Cora, Dylan. I really do, and that's why we're here. I was called back to work for an emergency, and honestly, I should be hightailing it back this moment, but I couldn't leave her, and I sure as fuck wouldn't dare take her from you without your blessing." Brett's words came out shaky, and I knew it took every ounce of courage he had.

"So, you skip out on me with our amazing business idea, move to California, never call, and then steal my nineteen-year-old daughter. Damn, you're a great friend."

Brett's muscles tensed, and he took a step forward. Unsure of his actions, I stood between the both of them and folded my arms across my chest. Perching on the edge of a stool, Brett placed his elbows on the center island and rubbed the back of his neck.

"First of all, I'm not stealing Cora. I might be many things, but a kidnapper, I am not. Secondly..." He trailed off and rested his eyes on me.

When I nodded gently, he released a shaky breath before combing his hands down the middle of his face. He promised on the ride back that he would be honest with Dad and finally tell him why he drove a wedge between them.

"Something got your tongue?" Dad snapped.

"I had every intention of starting up the garage

with you, but the closer we got to making our dream a reality, the closer I was pushed into a corner, caged by fear and…the real reason why I skipped out is that I didn't want us to turn out like our dads. I was—"

"Our dads?" Dylan interjected.

Brett nodded. "Yeah. You know what happened between our dads with the CD company they tried to get off the ground. It ruined their friendship and…"

"No shit, Sherlock. Our dads tried selling faulty CD players to anyone who had two eyes, a mouth, and cash in their pocket. They both were quacks, and that was no business."

"Um, what's a CD player?" I asked and placed my hands on my hip.

They both broke out in unexpected laughter, and Brett pulled me into his embrace and placed a soft kiss on my forehead. Running his hands through my hair, he inhaled me and tightened his grip around my waist.

"So, you two really are…a thing? You do know she's nineteen, right?" Dad said while mimicking my age with his fingers.

Brett reached for a pear and rolled it around in his hand. "Yes, but she's amazing. She's smart, beautiful, resourceful, and has just as much attitude as you. I'm crazy about her, Dylan."

"I lose a girlfriend, and you gain a lover. Well, I did fall in love with your mother after 48 hours, so, like father like daughter, eh?" Dad joked while shaking his head.

I turned, pressing my back into Brett's hard chest as I dug my toe into the grooves of the kitchen tile. For the first time the air didn't feel so stiff, and a small smile peeked from under my dad's beard.

"Water under the bridge?" Brett asked as he rocked me in his arms.

Dad tossed the beer bottle in the recycle bin and closed the gap between us. "How about we rebuild the bridge. Maybe this time around, you'll have the balls to cross it."

Printed in Great Britain
by Amazon